PRAISE FOR

What newspapers say

"She keeps company with the best mystery writers" – *The Times*

"LJ Ross is the queen of Kindle" – *Sunday Telegraph*

"Holy Island is a blockbuster" – *Daily Express*

"A literary phenomenon" – *Evening Chronicle*

"A pacey, enthralling read" – *Independent*

What readers say

"I couldn't put it down. I think the full series will cause a divorce, but it will be worth it."

"I gave this book 5 stars because there's no option for 100."

"Thank you, LJ Ross, for the best two hours of my life."

"This book has more twists than a demented corkscrew."

"Another masterpiece in the series. The DCI Ryan mysteries are superb, with very realistic characters and wonderful plots. They are a joy to read!"

BOOKS BY LJ ROSS

THE ALEXANDER GREGORY THRILLERS:

1. *Impostor*
2. *Hysteria*
3. *Bedlam*
4. *Mania*
5. *Panic*
6. *Amnesia*

THE DCI RYAN MYSTERIES:

1. *Holy Island*
2. *Sycamore Gap*
3. *Heavenfield*
4. *Angel*
5. *High Force*
6. *Cragside*
7. *Dark Skies*
8. *Seven Bridges*
9. *The Hermitage*
10. *Longstone*
11. *The Infirmary (Prequel)*
12. *The Moor*
13. *Penshaw*
14. *Borderlands*
15. *Ryan's Christmas*
16. *The Shrine*
17. *Cuthbert's Way*
18. *The Rock*
19. *Bamburgh*
20. *Lady's Well*
21. *Death Rocks*
22. *Poison Garden*
23. *Belsay*

THE SUMMER SUSPENSE MYSTERIES:

1. *The Cove*
2. *The Creek*
3. *The Bay*
4. *The Haven*

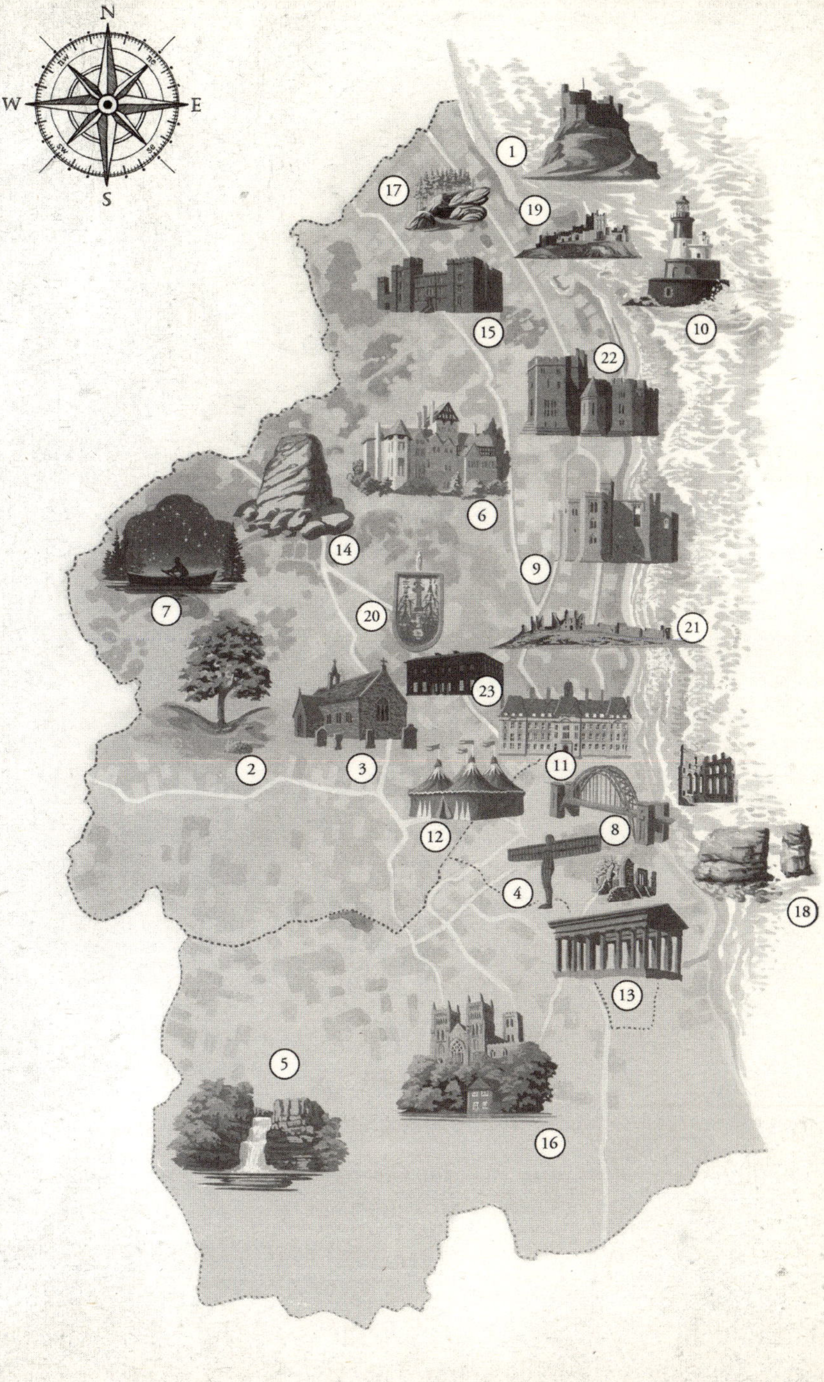
N
W
E
S
nw
ne
sw
se
1
2
3
4
5
6
7
8
9
10
11
12
13
14
15
16
17
18
19
20
21
22
23

BELSAY

A DCI RYAN MYSTERY

BELSAY

A DCI RYAN MYSTERY

LJ ROSS

This is a work of fiction. Names, characters, businesses, places, events and incidents are either the products of the author's imagination or used in a fictitious manner. Any resemblance to actual persons, living or dead, or actual events is purely coincidental.

ISBN: 978-1-912310-23-4

First published in March 2025 by Dark Skies Publishing

Author photo by Gareth Iwan Jones

Cover artwork and map by Andrew Davidson

Cover layout and typesetting by
Riverside Publishing Solutions Limited

Printed and bound in Great Britain by Clays Ltd, Elcograf S.p.A.

FSC
www.fsc.org
MIX
Paper | Supporting responsible forestry
FSC® C018072

For my children

PROLOGUE

Belsay Hall
Christmas Eve, 1890

"Your guests will be arriving shortly, sir."

William Edgington, eighth baronet of that ancient name, continued to inspect his cravat in the looking glass. He turned this way and that, admiring his reflection much like Narcissus—though, thankfully, without the additional hazard of a deep pool of water, into which he would undoubtedly have fallen. His valet, a tall, thin-faced man of indeterminate middle age known simply as 'Porter', waited patiently and adopted a neutral expression which masked any private opinions he might have held about his master being a spoilt young ass.

"—my wife?"

Porter came to attention. "I beg your pardon, sir?"

Edgington caught his valet's eye in the mirror. "I dislike having to repeat myself," he snapped, and looked down his patrician nose at a man who was old enough to be his father, and wiser by far.

"I'm terribly sorry, sir. It won't happen again."

Edgington sniffed. "See that it doesn't," he said, turning back to his visage. "I *asked* whether my wife has left her rooms?"

"I believe Lady Edgington is already downstairs, sir, preparing to greet your guests."

William retrieved a shining gold pocket watch from his waistcoat, checked the hour, and performed a swift calculation.

Not enough time to get there and back again.

Aware that Porter was watching him from beneath the hoods of his wrinkled eyelids, he rearranged his handsome face into its usual hauteur and smoothed his blond hair, allowing a rakish curl to dip over his forehead. Immensely satisfied, he gave a brief nod, and his manservant stepped forward with an elegant black dinner jacket which he slid gently over his arms. Finally, Porter reached for a set of pristine white gloves which he presented to the baronet on a silver platter.

Edgington tugged the silk over his hands, and flexed his fingers like a cat. "Inform my wife I'll join her directly."

"Very good, sir."

Lady Gertrude Edgington was the only daughter of a fabulously wealthy man.

Arthur Dodds had crossed the Atlantic and made a fortune before his thirtieth birthday, but his heart had always remained in Northumberland, where he was born the fifth of nine children to an unprosperous cattle farmer and his wife. The day after his sixteenth birthday, he'd taken himself down to the docks, where he'd stolen a rich man's cigarette case and exchanged it for passage with the bosun of a merchant vessel bound for the Americas. It had been an arduous journey on the high seas, but, the moment his feet touched New England soil, he hadn't stopped working; scrimping, saving, wheeling and dealing until he'd made himself a veritable mountain of gold. So much so that, upon his return to England twenty years later, he'd used some of it to purchase a large estate on the outskirts of Morpeth, a stone's throw from the modest farmstead he'd ploughed and tilled as a boy. He'd married the only daughter of the estate's impecunious local aristocrat—understanding correctly that, when climbing the ladder of Victorian society, the British were more often concerned with one's lineage than with their bank balance, though a little of both was ideal. Thus, he'd wedded himself to the drab but immensely grateful Miss Emily Greyson, and had approached the task of bedding her with as much enthusiasm as he could muster, until his wife informed him that she was with child. The matter of propagation reasonably settled, Arthur turned his attention back to social elevation and, after some extensive brown-nosing and private greasing of wheels, he managed to persuade The Powers That Be to bestow upon him a knighthood.

Sir Arthur Dodds had a lovely ring to it, he'd always thought.

Following the untimely death of his wife shortly after Gertrude's birth, and some initial disappointment that she was not the son he'd hoped for, Arthur soon became an indulgent father as well as a *very* indulgent patron to the many young dancers and actresses he entertained in his London townhouse. For a while, he deceived himself that he was looking for a second wife, and mother to his virginal daughter, who remained in Northumberland, safely beyond the reach of the many gold-digging dandies who circled like vultures. As an added precaution, he paid a small army of governesses and companions to watch over her in his absence, and report back to him with anything of concern.

Evidently, he hadn't paid them enough.

Arthur blamed himself for having underestimated the charms of young William Edgington, eldest son of the late baronet, whose family seat at Belsay was in danger of ruination thanks to successive patriarchs having run through the family's coffers with feckless abandon. Thus, the heir apparent found himself saddled with an ancient name, a dwindling line of credit, and an estate on the brink of bankruptcy. With only his personal charms to recommend himself, William understood that he needed to make a very good match; preferably, with a girl of 'good stock' but beggars could not be choosers. When one of his old Cambridge friends told him of the pretty, impressionable and *enormously* rich Miss Gertrude Dodds, who spent much of her time at home with her companions and knew little of men or of life beyond the pages of a Gothic romance novel, William rubbed his avaricious hands together and set about winning her over by fair means or foul.

Of course, the moment he'd caught wind of it, Arthur had known what the young man was about. William Edgington was far too handsome by half, whereas his Gertie—though quietly attractive and raised with all the airs and graces one would expect of a debutante—was hardly possessed of the kind of face or figure likely to turn heads.

He loves me, Papa! Gertie had wailed, after her father's discovery of their clandestine meetings, which only served to prove that the young man had no honour, nor any regard for her welfare or reputation.

And yet…

His daughter would be the wife of a baronet, and his grandson the heir.

"You both have my blessing," Dodds had gushed, in an abrupt turnaround that left Gertrude momentarily stunned, if not a little suspicious. "Send him to see me, and I'll shake his hand."

And so, the deal was done.

A little over a year since she'd said, 'I do' and taken up her new place in society, Gertrude paced around the drawing room of Belsay Hall while she sipped a glass of Madeira to calm her nerves. The hall was a relatively new addition to the estate, having been erected seventy years before in a neo-Classical style by her husband's father, at considerable expense. The old Mediaeval castle still stood nearby, weathered and crumbling like an Arcadian folly, and she thought it vastly more romantic an edifice, being smaller and built of thick stone covered in creeping ivy, its battlements scarred by the elements and its hallways oozing with history. However, she admitted, it was a draughty old place and much too small for a modern family…

The word *family* caused a small flutter in the region of her heart, though it could just as easily be attributed to the boned corset she wore, which had been sewn mercilessly tight in an effort to achieve the exaggerated hourglass figure that was the fashion of the day, and which was becoming more and more difficult to achieve as the baby grew steadily larger inside her womb. Gertrude tugged absent-mindedly at the sleeve of her heavy silk gown, which was a flattering shade of mulberry red trimmed with black lace that was apparently all the *rage* in London. She felt compelled to keep up with fashion, not only because she was now an important lady in the district and it was expected, but because she knew William would expect it, too. He was always so well-dressed—as handsome as a fairytale prince, or so the other ladies seemed at pains to remark upon at every social occasion, as though she, his wife, would have no feeling upon the matter. As it was, she could hardly believe William had chosen her from all the other girls he might have had. If she was surprised by how little time they spent together, or by his immediate loss of ardour following their marital vows, she put it down to his upbringing or the stress that came with his responsibility as master of all he surveyed. Besides which, as he'd told her many times, she knew very little of men.

Gertrude set her glass down on a nearby table and cast her eye over the rich furnishings laid out in the enormous drawing room—velvet chaises and draperies, oil paintings and chandeliers fitted with modern electric lighting, which was a new-fangled luxury. She'd baulked at the expense, but William had been adamant that their home be decked out like a palace and, she supposed, they could afford it. Perhaps she might have liked to see some of her dowry being spent on repairs to the farm-workers cottages, but, when she'd tried to raise the matter, William had forcibly reminded her that she was merely a *woman,* and it was not a woman's place to tell a *man* how to run his affairs.

Her eyes glazed with unexpected tears, which she blinked away rapidly.

"My lady?"

Her hand flew to her breast. "*Smythe,*" she said, with a nervous laugh for the elderly butler who hovered across the room. "I'm afraid I didn't hear you come in."

"I do apologise—" the butler began, in deferential tones.

She waved that away. "Is my husband ready? The guests will be here at any moment."

"I'm informed by his valet that Sir William will join you directly, ma'am. I wished to enquire whether the preparations meet with your ladyship's approval?"

She looked again at her surroundings, resplendent in shades of green, red and gold, and thought of the large fir tree sitting in the columned hallway; of the roaring fires lit in every room; of the dining table laden with all manner of luxurious food, and of the cellar filled with champagne ordered in by her husband.

Only the best for you, my turtle dove, he liked to say.

And for himself, of course, for he knew she couldn't stomach the bubbles in her condition.

She forced a smile, which was all bravado.

"Everything is perfect, Smythe," she replied, kindly. "Please convey my thanks to the staff, and I hope they liked their gifts?"

Earlier in the day, she'd made her way to the servant's hall armed with boxes of small Christmas presents wrapped in fine paper, as well a couple of under-maids bearing sugared sweets and oranges, a few books and an assortment of other items which were trifles to her but enormous treats to their intended recipients. William hadn't liked the idea, of course, preferring not to spoil 'the help' and compromise what he called, 'the distinction of rank'. To her shame, she'd defied him, and chosen to thank their servants personally. The bonus pay had been gratefully received, as well; something else she'd funded from the household expense sheet, since her own monies had been swiftly commandeered by her new husband, upon whom she was now entirely reliant.

"The staff were *most* grateful," Smythe assured her, and there was genuine warmth in his tone of address. He might have had his reservations about the daughter of a cloth merchant, but had been pleasantly surprised by the girl's firm but fair manner, not to mention her generous spirit. "Thank you again, my lady. It means a lot, at this time of year."

She nodded, then pressed a hand to her blooming stomach beneath the restrictive garments.

"Are you quite well—?" Smythe took a step forward.

"I—no, I'm fine, really. It was only the baby, making himself known."

Smythe gave her a fatherly smile. "It might be a daughter, yet. I'm told they give their mothers the most trouble."

Gertrude managed a laugh, and wished she could have known her own mother. Then, the smile faded as she remembered William's remarks about preferring a son, at all costs.

"Either will be a blessing to me," she said softly, and rubbed her stomach again. "So long as they're healthy."

Smythe bowed his head a little lower than was strictly necessary, in a mark of esteem. "I believe the first guests are arriving, if your ladyship will excuse me."

She nodded, and sucked in a trembling breath.

Where was William?

Just then, she heard his booming voice echo around the hallway outside.

"Gertrude! Where are you?"

She polished off the last of her Madeira in two gulps, dabbed the edge of her mouth with a laced handkerchief, and moved swiftly to the door.

"Iris! I'll be off now."

A short distance from Belsay Hall, Iris Webster looked up from her darning needles and smiled genially at her husband, who was one of several tenant farmers on the Belsay estate. Fred was a big lug of a man, but he was kind to her and worshipped the ground she walked on.

"All right, my love," she said. "Enjoy yourself."

"Don't wait up for me," Fred said, and shrugged into his heavy wool coat. "It'll be late, by the time I make my way back from the pub."

She was counting on it, Iris thought.

"I'll make up a plate for you, in case you're peckish once you come home," she said.

Fred gave her a broad smile and thought, not for the first time, that he was the luckiest of men. His wife was not only a great beauty, with her dark hair and porcelain skin…not to mention the voluptuous curves hidden beneath the stiff dress she wore which only *he* was ever allowed to see. More than this, she wasn't like any of the other farmer's wives, nagging him about this or that, or telling him to hurry back from the pub on Christmas Eve. He was the envy of all his friends and acquaintances, and he thanked God for sending her to him.

Fred surprised himself by leaning down to kiss her upturned face.

"What was that for?" she asked.

Embarrassed to say it, but compelled nonetheless, Fred gave an awkward shrug of his bear-like shoulders. "I—I love you, lass. That's all."

Iris swallowed a hard ball of guilt. "Oh, get away with you," she said breezily, and shooed him off. "Before you go soft in the head!"

"Aye," he agreed, with a good-natured chuckle. "Is the lad asleep?"

Iris thought of her five-year-old son, who slept soundly in his room upstairs, and nodded.

"Don't go wakin' him up, when you roll back in here at yon time of the mornin'," she warned him, but softened the words with a wink.

Fred nodded and, tugging a cap over his ears, headed out into the night.

Iris waited for another half an hour, then set aside her mending and hurried upstairs to the topmost bedroom in the farmhouse. It was intended for a scullery maid, but it had been a long time since they'd been able to afford any help inside the house, so the room stood empty and cold but for a rocking chair, a single candlestick and a small box of matches on the windowsill. Spying them, she crossed the floorboards, which creaked beneath her weight, and lit the candle. She stood there for a moment, looking out across the fields towards the main hall, where the windows glowed brightly, and the sound of music and chatter carried across the paddock.

One day, she thought, and her lips curved into a smile.

She made her way back downstairs and settled down by the fire to wait.

"Well, ladies, I believe it's time for us to withdraw, and leave our gentlemen to their cigars."

Gertrude rose from her chair and the other ladies seated around the long, polished dining table followed her lead. Their husbands and fathers half-rose, then fell back down again, their bellies pleasantly full of wine and game pie. Only when the door closed behind their women, who left in a cloud of floral perfume and rustling skirts, did the *real* talk begin.

"Splendid little filly you've caught there, Edgington," one of them remarked, once the cigars had been lit and the port decanted. "Meek as a lamb, and not too bad to look at, either."

The baronet inclined his head. "Especially in this light," he said, unkindly. "But then, we only tend to see one another in the hours of darkness."

There was a rumble of laughter around the table.

"Money looks good, whatever the hour," another man quipped, and they all laughed again.

"I'll toast to that," Edgington said, and raised his glass. "To our wives, and their beautiful dowries."

The men clinked glasses, and drank.

After a few minutes' token discussion of business, of local gossip and farming thereabouts, they moved on to more important matters.

"What d'you say to a game of backgammon, Edgington? It's been at least two weeks since I lightened your pockets."

William opened his mouth to reply, but the sound died on his lips as he caught the flicker of a light burning through the trees across the lawn, in the window of the nearest tenant farmhouse.

He stubbed out his cigar.

"I'll join you all in the library shortly," he said briskly, and raised a finger to his butler. "Our discussion has reminded me of a small matter of business I must attend to, which cannot wait. I shan't be long."

Smythe crossed the room to his master's side and leaned down so he could hear the words spoken beneath Edgington's breath.

"Tell Porter to go and knock on the door," he said. "He'll know what that means."

Smythe thought of the pregnant young woman holding court in the adjoining room, and his lips pressed together in disapproval. “Yes, sir. Will that be all?”

“See that our guests have everything they need whilst I’m gone.”

“Very good, sir.”

With that, William excused himself and retreated to the hallway, leaving his friends to continue working their way through his wine cellar. He dodged the grand, fluted columns which had been inspired by his father’s many trips to Greece and Italy, and made his way out of the front door. In the early days, he might have thought to use the game larder door or some other more discreet exit, but he was *master* of Belsay, and the master could do whatever he damn well pleased.

That being said, he was careful to keep to the shadows of the house as he skirted around towards the stables, passing beneath an impressive clock tower which chimed the hour. He knew the lady’s husband to be a gentle sort, by all accounts, but Frederick Webster was built like a brick shithouse, so it seemed prudent not to arouse his anger. The moon shone bright that night, illuminating the paddocks and the passing figure of Porter, his manservant, who was already making his return journey from the direction of the Webster farmhouse, his shoes crunching against the gravel on the estate’s winding driveway. William watched until his valet disappeared beyond the edge of the house and then, as a cloud passed over the moon, he darted along the carriage driveway and soon after disappeared into the bowels of the earth under the cover of darkness.

March 1891 – three months later
Office of the Chief Constable of Northumberland

"Mr Webster, this *is* a pleasant surprise."

The Chief Constable of the newly-formed Northumberland County Police Constabulary was exercising a healthy degree of sarcasm, for it was well known that Webster—who was coming to be known as 'Funny Farm Fred' to the bobbies thereabouts—made it his business to darken the Chief Constable's door on a regular weekly basis.

"Have you—"

"*No,*" the Chief Constable snapped, and sat in his desk chair with an audible *thud*. "As I've told you many times before, your wife is nowhere to be found. I've put search parties out…the whole blasted county has. We've combed rivers, hills, alleyways, hospitals—" *And mortuaries,* he almost said, before catching himself. "There's simply been no trace of her, Webster. I'm sorry for it, but we have plenty of other cases and limited men to deal with them. You really must buck up, now, and accept the possibility that—*ah*—Iris, was it?"

His eyes dropped to the file in front of him, where her name had been written in neat, curving script.

"Yes, *Iris*," he said to himself, before looking again at the quiet hulk of a man across the table from him. "Some women find the country life too tame, y' know. Who's to say a travelling man didn't spin her some yarn or other about treading the boards in London, or being an artist's muse? Maybe your wife wanted a new life for herself, after all."

Captain Herbert Durrell Terry came from a long line of military men. As such, he believed in the rigours of self-discipline, on and off the battlefield. In his role as Chief Constable of the county constabulary, he was an exacting man who elicited results, though there were always exceptions and, it seemed, the case of Iris Webster was to be one of them. A rare beauty of a woman, she'd gone missing on the night of Christmas Eve, not three months before, leaving her young child sleeping alone in the family's farmhouse while her husband was with his circle of friends at the local drinking hole—which he went to infrequently, but often on Friday evenings along with many a working man. Nobody at Belsay claimed to know a thing about the matter, including the Edgington family, whom he'd been loath to bother with such a matter, but it was necessary as a matter of strict procedure. His constables had interviewed any number of farm workers and serving staff who worked on the Belsay estate where her husband kept his farm, but they appeared to be as surprised as her husband was to return home from the pub and find Iris missing.

As for Webster, he'd come dressed in his smartest tweed suit which hung more limply from his bones than it had done when he'd first raised the alarm. Terry admired a man who presented himself well regardless of social position, and thought idly that Webster would have made an excellent addition to his former regiment, but that was neither here nor there. Had it not been for the farmer's mild and softly spoken manner, he might have looked more closely at his motivations, considering how frequently these things ended up being a domestic matter.

"Iris—Iris would never've left our John," Fred ventured to say. "Even if—if she was sick o' livin' the farm life, with me, she'd never've left our John."

That also had the ring of truth to it, Terry had to admit. It appeared that their friends and neighbours had been universal in remarking that Iris Webster was a doting mother to the couple's only son, and that the boy was quite a cherub, with his blond hair and blue eyes.

Blond hair, blue eyes, he repeated to himself.

The man standing in front of him was possessed of unremarkable, mid-brown hair, and brown eyes; as for Iris Webster, he knew her to have been blessed with striking dark looks, which was certainly true if the black and white photograph of her was anything to go by. It showed the couple on their wedding day, she seated stiffly in bridal white, while her husband towered above her in a dark suit, sporting a carnation in his lapel and a gawkish smile on his face which seemed to convey his bemusement at having married such a woman.

"They can be strange creatures," Terry said, half to himself.

"I beg your pardon, sir?" Webster asked him, and Terry tugged at his moustache before leaning forward in his desk chair to speak man-to-man. "Now, look, old chap. No man likes to think of his wife having…well, you know, *put it about*. But, it would hardly be the first time a beautiful woman like Iris had her head turned, now, would it?"

Webster turned sheet white, then shook his head side to side while his hands curled into fists. "Iris wasn't like that," he managed, keeping his anger tightly in check.

Captain Terry approved of that, too, for it confirmed his assessment. Webster had a good degree of self-control, even when provoked, which made it unlikely he'd have lost his temper and battered the poor woman to death.

Which still didn't leave them any closer to discovering her whereabouts…

"All right, man. *All right*," he said, in archly patrician tones. "I've written to colleagues across the land, and there's every chance she'll turn up once she realises her mistake. Everyone's entitled to one bit of tomfoolery, eh?" He tried a touch of levity, which fell on profoundly deaf ears.

"She didn't take any of her clothes," Fred argued. "Why wouldn't Iris take some clothes, if she was plannin' to leave?"

"Well, God help us, Webster, do *any* of us know how the female mind works?" Terry blustered. "It makes no sense to men of the world such as ourselves...but a woman in *hysterics*, prone to impulsive action...now, that's something you and I couldn't possibly comprehend." He shook his head, sadly, and his impressive moustache twitched as if to punctuate the point. "It's just as likely your wife had a fancy to see the big city lights, to go to a variety show or some such, and, knowing you'd never agree to pack up and leave, she threw in the towel and headed off into the night with nothing but the bare necessities. Can you really be sure of what she did or didn't take?"

Webster looked down at his hands. "No," he whispered. "I didn't pay enough attention to her."

"There you have it," Captain Terry said. "Now, there's no need for you to keep coming all the way out to see me here. As soon as I, or any of the constabulary officers, hear the first thing about Iris, we'll gallop straight over to see you. How's that?"

But there was just one more thing Fred needed to say. "I've been thinkin'," he said quietly. "What if Iris isn't missin'?"

The Chief Constable frowned in confusion. "What d'you mean?"

"I mean to say, what if somethin'...or someone's hurt her?"

The Chief Constable looked squarely into the farmer's ruddy, trusting face, and wished he could tell him it was unlikely, or that young women like Iris didn't come a cropper and end up dumped in a ditch somewhere. Unfortunately, he couldn't tell him anything of the sort, for it would be untrue. If there was a chance that Iris Webster had moved to a city down south, changed her name and was now dancing a jig or warming some other feller's bed, there was an equal if not more likely chance that she was lying in a shallow grave or in a river bed.

"Best to leave the investigation to us," was all he said, and rose from his chair to show Webster the door. "Take my advice and turn your mind to looking after that boy of yours."

Fred thought of his son, John. "Aye," he said, gruffly. "Iris would want that."

While Fred made his way back from the Chief Constable's office, five-year-old John helped to care for the horses with one of Edgington's groomsmen, who happened to be a good friend of his father's.

"You can give Bessie a rub down, now, if you've a mind to."

John nodded eagerly, and took a brush from the groom, slipping his small fingers beneath the leather strap and stepping up onto a wooden stool so that he could reach the horse's mane. 'Bessie' was a beautiful Arabian mare with rich chestnut colouring, and a sweet temper to match her rider.

"This is Lady Edgington's horse," the groom explained to his young charge. "She's a gentle one, which is lucky for her ladyship, since she's no natural rider, God bless 'er."

John continued to brush the mare's back in long strokes, which the horse tolerated happily.

"Mistress can't ride 'er at the moment, anyhow," the man continued, as if he was chatting to one of his fellow hands and not a five-year-old who didn't care, either way. "She's confined, so they say. Got a baby comin'—next in line to all this, if it's a boy."

John's eyes burned with tears, as he thought of his own mother. "Do you—do you know where my mother's gone?" he asked softly.

The groom thought of Iris Webster, a girl who'd never been suited to life on a farm, and who'd abandoned Fred and their boy while she went off in search of better things.

Rumour was, she'd had her eye on the master...

He struggled to think of something tactful to say, and was grateful for a reprieve.

"Thomas? I thought I'd come and say 'hello' to Bessie, before I grow too big to waddle anywhere—oh! You've got company today, I see."

"Good afternoon, m' lady," Thomas said, and tipped his cap. When John said nothing, and merely stood on his little stool with the brush suspended mid-air, he gave the lad a stern look. "*John,* show her ladyship some respect—"

The boy seemed to remember he was supposed to defer to his 'betters', although the woman who stood before him didn't look too different to his mother, albeit she had finer clothes and a fancy hat perched on top of her head.

"Beg pardon, m' lady," he whispered, shyly.

Charmed by the small boy, Gertrude reached out to ruffle his hair. "You're forgiven," she said, with an impish smile. "I see you're taking very good care of my horse, so I think that should earn you a slice of cake in the kitchen. What do you say, young man?"

His blue eyes shone with happiness. "Yes, please," he whispered again, and turned to Thomas. "If—if I'm allowed?"

"It's up to her ladyship, lad. Mind you thank Cook, and come straight back 'ere after."

John nodded vigorously, then took Gertrude's outstretched hand, marvelling at how soft her palm felt without its glove. His mother, though as lovely as a queen, so his father said, had calloused hands from hours of washing and scrubbing, but this lady's hands were smooth as butter.

"What are you doing?"

All three turned at the unexpected sound of Sir Edgington's voice, which cracked like a whip. He was framed in the stable doorway, dressed for riding with a hat under the crook of his arm, and wore a dangerous expression.

"Hello, my dear," Gertrude said, a bit nervously. "I was just inviting this young gentleman for cake in the kitchen, since he's taken such good care of the horses, today—"

"You'll do *no such thing*," William ground out. "Return to the house, immediately."

Gertrude was stunned. "William, I don't understand—"

"*Do as your husband commands*," he snarled. "You shouldn't be walking around the estate in your condition, in any case. Do you want to endanger our unborn child? Now, do as I say and *return to the house*."

Confused, humiliated, Gertrude found the courage to turn to the little boy and muster a smile. "We'll have some cake another time," she said softly.

But, as she looked down into his rounded face, the truth struck her then, like a thunderbolt.

Blond hair, blue eyes, and the same even features as her husband…

She turned to look at William again, and her mouth fell open.

The likeness was uncanny.

"I—I—" she stuttered, looking between them while her brain struggled to compute what her eyes could see, all too clearly.

"Thomas? Lady Edgington feels unwell," William said, interpreting the reason for her sudden pallor. "Escort her back to the house and I'll be along in a moment."

"Yes, sir."

The groom took Gertrude's arm, and she leaned heavily upon him as he led her from the stables. Once she was out of earshot, the baronet surveyed his son with atavistic pride and took a couple of involuntary steps forward, though he knew it was foolish to be led by sentiment. Still, his own vanity enjoyed seeing the fruit of his labours in the boy that stood before him, who was already tall for his age, with the handsome features that would develop into a carbon copy of his own, in twenty years' time.

"Can I help you, sir?" John asked, feeling uncomfortable beneath the scrutiny, and a little frightened, though the master hadn't done or said anything untoward. All the same, there was something behind his eyes he didn't like; something he had no means to convey, except to say it was an instinctive feeling that a young, vulnerable animal might feel in the presence of a fully-grown lion.

"I'm sorry about your mother," William said quietly, and the boy looked down at his feet, to hide his tears.

"She's comin' back," he said, stubbornly, and swiped at his nose with the back of his sleeve. "They say she isn't, but she is. I *know* she is."

William continued to watch the boy in silence, then retrieved something from his inner pocket. "Here," he said, brusquely. "Take this."

He held out his gold pocket watch, which had been engraved with his father's and grandfather's names, as well as his own. Three generations of Edgington men had possessed that watch and now, in a manner of speaking, the fourth would possess it, too.

John looked at the timepiece. "I—I can't take that, sir, my father wouldn't like it."

"Take it," William insisted, and thrust the watch into the boy's pocket. "Oh, and, believe me, your father will approve." He smiled at the private joke, which wasn't in very good taste. "Mind you keep it to yourself and don't show anyone, or they'll think you've stolen it," he added.

John felt the weight of the watch in his trouser pocket, and hardly knew what to say. "Th—thank you, sir."

William gave the ghost of a smile. "Let's call it something to remember me by," he said quietly, and began to reach out his hand again, possibly to brush the boy's head, as Gertrude had done.

But then, he snatched it back.

"Give my regards to your father," he said.

With that, he turned on his heel and strode out of the stables.

CHAPTER 1

Belsay Hall, Northumberland
20th December 2024

"This narf beat the pub for a work night out!"

Detective Sergeant Frank Phillips made this declaration as he and an assortment of friends and colleagues from the Northumbria Police Constabulary walked the short distance from the visitors' car park to the main entrance of Belsay Hall. It was a beautiful country house in the Northumbrian countryside, built in the early nineteenth century in Greek-revival style for the Edgington family and situated to the west of the city of Newcastle upon Tyne, not too far from the constabulary's former headquarters. Snow had fallen sometime during the day, and its manicured lawns were covered in a blanket of white which glimmered beneath the light of the moon, while strings of festoon lights illuminated the pathways and columns to guide them through the wintry night.

"Until ten minutes ago, you were still complaining about the fact we wouldn't be having our Christmas party at the pub, this year."

This came from Detective Inspector Denise MacKenzie, who was both a stickler for detail and a bloodhound for sniffing out the truth, both of which she employed professionally as Phillips' senior officer, not to mention privately, as his wife and unofficial Enforcer of Biscuit Rations and Arbiter of Stottie Cake Consumption in the MacKenzie-Phillips household.

"Now, I never said I didn't like the look o' the place," he argued. "All I said was that I didn't understand why the Chief was puttin' on all these airs and graces, when a pie and a pint has been good enough for the likes of us every other year."

Chief Constable Sandra Morrison, who happened to be walking a few paces ahead of him, craned her neck around to fix him with her beady eye, which he could barely make out in the surrounding darkness, but could still feel as keenly as a laser beam. "Keep at it, Frank, and you'll be *lucky* to get a pie or a pint," she purred. "But, since you mention it, I booked to have our Christmas party here at Belsay because it's a lovely setting and I thought we could all use a treat, to celebrate the end of a hard year. That last case was trying for *all* of us, so it's about time we got dressed up and let our hair down—well, most of us, that is."

She eyed Phillips' thinning crop of salt-and-pepper grey hair.

"Here, now, watch it," he said, with the kind of ease that came of long friendship. "There's plenty of famous actors without much on top, y'nah. Take Jason Statham… Billy Zane…that bloke from *The King and I*…"

"Yul Brynner?" Morrison queried, in disbelief. "The man passed away donkey's years ago. Do you have any more recent examples of fetching baldies?"

Phillips lifted his chin, and prayed for divine inspiration. "Actually, well…alreet, alreet, give us a minute…*aye*! Aye, howay then, what about Jude Law, eh? You can't tell me the man isn't a candidate for a Turkish hair transplant—"

"I don't think anyone looks at his hair, sarge," one of the female constables threw in, and they all laughed. "They're too busy looking at his other attributes."

"Well, that just proves my point," Phillips said. "Besides, I've never had any complaints from the lasses—"

"Which *lasses* would they be?" his wife intoned, and Phillips could almost feel the noose tightening around his neck.

He laughed, nervously, and gave the tall, raven-haired man who walked beside him a desperate nudge. "Help us out," he muttered.

Detective Chief Inspector Maxwell Finley-Ryan grinned, his teeth flashing white in the surrounding gloom. "Sorry Frank," he said. "I'd take a bullet for your daft old arse, but I won't stand between an Irishwoman and her idiot husband. D'you think I have a death wish?"

There was another ripple of laughter amongst the crowd, while Phillips pursed his lips.

"I agree with the Chief, though," Ryan continued, as they neared the entrance steps to the hall. "This does make a nice change, after the time we've had. I think we could all use a break from murder, just for tonight."

"Well, *now* you've done it." The words were spoken by the slim, dark-haired woman who walked by his side.

"What have I done?" he asked his wife.

"You've tempted fate," Anna told him, sagely. "You said the words all of us were thinking, but were too canny to say aloud. Now, I wouldn't be surprised if a body falls right onto our dinner plates."

"It's the southerner in him," Phillips put in. "He doesn't have a healthy respect for superstition, like we do up north."

"Here I was, relying on logic and reason, when all I had to do was carry a rabbit's foot in my pocket," the southerner said.

"Aye, and that explains why I've had to get you out of so many scrapes over the years."

Ryan opened his mouth to argue but, to his chagrin, he realised that Phillips *had* been there for him more often than not, and usually in circumstances when reason or logic had played no part in the situation whatsoever.

"Should I be making a note of these insightful nuggets?" This came from the newest member of the Major Crimes Division, Detective Constable Charlie Reed.

She was a recent transfer from their regional office in Alnwick, and was keen to learn from the knowledge and experience of Ryan and his team—a journey which began, first and foremost, with an understanding of the art of sarcasm, it seemed.

"You're best off ignoring these two halfwits," the Chief Constable threw back. "God knows why I keep them on the payroll."

In high spirits, Frank began to belt out a Bing Crosby medley, starting with *White Christmas* followed by *Little Drummer Boy,* while their feet crunched over the frosted gravel in time to the beat. His good humour was infectious and, soon enough, the rest of the department began to chip in with 'ba-rum-pa-pum-pum' at the appropriate moments, their voices echoing out into the night.

The merry tribe covered the remaining driveway until they reached the columned entrance to the hall, where they were greeted by the estate's Events Manager, a smart woman by the name of Barbara Elder, who smiled broadly and ushered them in through a set of heavy oak doors.

"Welcome to Belsay!" she said, cheerfully. "Come in, out of the cold, and warm yourselves with a glass of mulled wine!"

They murmured their thanks and stepped inside, rubbing their chilled hands together as they passed through a tiled entranceway and helped themselves to a glass of spiced wine from the serving staff who awaited them. Once fortified, they moved into a central, pillared atrium that vaguely resembled a Grecian temple, and gave access to the main rooms on the ground floor. An impressive stone staircase led from there to the first floor, around which was a galleried landing with a large glass cupula built into the ceiling overhead, to shine light down into the atrium during the day. Since it was now dark outside, the hall had been lit by numerous candles and electric lamps, as well as fairy lights woven through the gallery rails and up the stairs, setting off a beautiful array of yule-time garlands. In the corner, an enormous fir tree was decked in greens and reds, with more twinkling lights. In the centre of it all, a long dining table had been laid out, equally lit by the gentle glow of candlelight which bounced off the polished cutlery and shining glassware.

"This isn't the dining room, of course," Barbara said, gesturing to the table. "But, for larger events like these, this is a much more impressive space. You can really appreciate the architecture, from here."

Indeed, several uplighters had been positioned at the base of the surrounding pillars, and it reminded Ryan of a trip he'd once made to the Acropolis for a sound and light show one balmy evening when he was a younger man.

"It's lovely," he said, and meant it. "Do the Edgington family still live here?"

"The hall has been unoccupied for a number of years, since the last baronet died intestate," Barbara explained. "Since then, the estate has been run by a trust, who've maintained the house and grounds and tried to make the most of it, until an heir could be found through probate. Thankfully, a distant relative of the late baronet was uncovered quite recently, living in Australia—he's due to arrive any day now, to look things over. It'll be quite a change in circumstances for him, I imagine."

Ryan nodded, and wondered whether the new baronet knew what he'd be letting himself in for. As heir to a large estate himself, he'd grown up in its shadow and that of generations of 'Ryans of Summersley'. The thought of giving over his life to the running of such an entity was a daunting prospect, and one he didn't relish.

"I wish him well," he said, and excused himself to take his place at the table as a harpist began to pluck out the soft strains of a Northumbrian melody.

The table was a long oval covered in pristine white cloth, and the twenty or so attendees had been seated in a classic boy-girl formation, couples having deliberately been separated to encourage discussion with other people. Consequently, Ryan found himself between Chief Constable Morrison and an empty chair assigned to—

He checked the name card.

DC Melanie Yates.

She was nowhere to be seen, and a quick scan told him that Jack Lowerson, her boyfriend and fellow detective constable in Major Crimes, was also missing from the table.

Choosing not to speculate, Ryan continued to study the gathered assembly, pausing to smile at Anna, who was seated directly across from him nestled between

Frank Phillips and Tom Faulkner, their Senior Scenes of Crimes Officer. He might have been a consultant on paper, but Faulkner was an integral part of their team and deserved his seat at the table. The same could be said of the forensic pathologist, Jeffrey Pinter, who'd abandoned the morbidity of his day job in favour of the land of the living, for once, appearing sublimely happy to have found himself between an attractive intelligence analyst and the Chief Constable's personal assistant. As for Charlie Reed, she'd found herself on the other side of Frank Phillips, with an empty space beside her, which meant—

"Sorry we're late!" Detective Constable Jack Lowerson hurried into the atrium, the heels of his shoes clicking against the stone floor. Like the other men in the room, he wore formal black tie, while Detective Constable Melanie Yates was a bronzed beauty beside him, in a silk dress she'd picked up during her recent sabbatical in Thailand. Charlie looked up as they entered, then swiftly away again, reaching for her glass of wine.

"And here I was, thinking there wouldn't be any drama this evening," Morrison muttered, beneath her breath. "Whoever did the table plan deserves to be shot."

Ryan raised a questioning eyebrow.

"Don't tell me you haven't noticed the way Charlie looks at Jack—or, the way *he* looks at *her*, for that matter," Morrison hissed. "It's as plain as the nose on my face that the pair of them have feelings for one another. That was all well and good when Melanie was out of the picture, but she's back now, isn't she?"

Ryan watched in mute surprise as his friend took up the empty chair beside Charlie Reed, while Melanie made her way around the table to take her seat beside him, pausing to chat to another member of the team for a few precious moments.

"What are you, the Love Police?" he hissed back. "How d'you know *any* of this?"

"See for yourself!"

Morrison jerked her chin towards the other side of the table, where Jack and Charlie were now sitting beside one another with the kind of awkwardness that could only be emulated by a pair of high school kids who'd just been told they were pairing up for a ballroom dancing competition.

"Bloody hell," he said. "A love triangle is all we need."

"What have I missed?" Melanie asked, and plonked herself on the chair beside him.

Ryan exchanged a telling look with Morrison, then cleared his throat. "Booze," he said, succinctly. "I think that's what we're all missing."

CHAPTER 2

Twenty minutes later, the crowd of police personnel chattered happily over a main course of turkey with all the trimmings, or, in the case of Jack Lowerson, a vegetarian-friendly nut roast.

"Still claiming not to like meat, eh?" Charlie spoke the words shyly, as though meeting him for the first time. In many ways, it felt as though she was talking to a different Jack; there was the one who existed *before* Melanie Yates had returned home, who was uncommitted and beginning to open himself to the possibility of a relationship with someone else. Then, there was the one who existed *after* she'd returned, who remembered that he loved Mel, and all the happy times they'd spent together before trauma had driven a wedge between them. *That* Jack was a stranger to her, so Charlie had taken a step back, leaving them to rekindle their romance. It was the honourable thing to do, she told herself, and yet—

It hurt, she acknowledged.

It hurt to see Jack and Mel together, around the office.

It hurt to hear their easy banter, the shared stories and memories that were made long before she'd met either of them.

It hurt to see how easily Melanie had slipped back into the rhythm of the team, who'd welcomed her with open arms, as if she'd never been away nor caused any pain to those she'd left behind.

Most of all, it hurt to admit that, fundamentally, Mel was a nice person. She'd been through unspeakable trauma at the hands of a brutal killer, who was also responsible for murdering her twin sister, years before. It was hardly surprising she'd suffered a kind of breakdown, and it was only right that she should be met with kindness and understanding. In different circumstances, Charlie would have been the first to extend a hand in friendship, but instead, she kept a safe distance. She refused lunch dates and coffee breaks with her new colleague, on whatever pretext came to mind, because to cultivate a friendship with Melanie would only bring her closer to Jack, which wouldn't help matters at all.

Now, having been thrust beside one another at dinner, Charlie acknowledged that an evening spent in awkward silence would invite questions, not least from Jack himself.

And so she teased him, as she might have done any other member of the team.

"Yeah, that's still the cover story," he replied, and prodded a piece of the offending nut roast. "I try to have principles, but why the hell does nut roast have to taste so bad?"

She slathered cranberry sauce on her next forkful of turkey, and tried not to look as though she was relishing it too much. "It's the carnivore deep inside you, rebelling against it," she said. "Being a principled vegetarian seems a lot like being a recovering addict; you're not turning your back on meat because you don't like the taste."

"I still dream about bacon sandwiches, sometimes," he confessed.

Charlie laughed, drawing a knowing look from Denise, who was seated between a couple of colleagues a little further along from the Chief Constable, and whose position afforded an uninterrupted view of the pair of them. "Ever feel tempted?"

Jack turned to look at her sharply, taking in the lovely rust-coloured dress Charlie wore, and the way the light burnished her hair, then dragged his eyes away. He didn't answer the question and instead forced some more nut roast down his gullet. "So, ah, how's Ben doing? Still settling into the new place?"

Jack had helped Charlie and her young son, Ben, move into an apartment in Newcastle, so that she could take up her new position on Ryan's team. They'd become friends over the cardboard boxes and during the course of their last investigation, and she'd come to trust Jack enough to him introduce her son, who was her pride and joy and the reason why she worked so hard. As a single mother, she hadn't had the easiest few years but then, as she would have said herself, there was always someone who'd had a worse time of it. Her innate optimism matched his own, and was just one reason why they got along so well.

"Ben's doing well at his new nursery," she said, and a gentle, motherly smile teased the corners of her mouth. "He was one of the wise men in their nativity play, and he did an excellent job of stomping into the 'stable' to throw a bag of 'frankincense' at the baby Jesus. Thank goodness the manger wasn't occupied by a real baby, or there might have been a case for Grievous Bodily Harm."

It was Jack's turn to laugh, as he imagined Ben delivering his gift with all the finesse of a bull in a china shop.

"And your mum?" he asked. "How's she getting along?"

To add to her list of personal responsibilities, Charlie was a part-time carer to her mother, who'd been diagnosed with multiple sclerosis a couple of years before and, although still mobile, was beginning to suffer more serious effects of that cruel degenerative disease. To make life easier, Charlie had stretched her personal resources and invested in a pretty garden flat large enough for all three of them, so her mother could be close to family and receive any help she might need from her daughter, until more specialist care became necessary down the line.

"She's pretty stable, at the moment," Charlie replied, and dabbed at her lips with a napkin. "I worry about her, but she's on the right medication and she has a physiotherapy session once a week. I think it should be more frequent, but…" She shrugged, too proud to admit they couldn't afford to pay for additional private sessions.

Jack wasn't fooled, and, without thinking, he put a warm hand over hers. "You're doing all you can," he said, and squeezed her fingers in support.

She looked down at their hands, then moved hers away. "Jack—"

"Charlie—"

"Sorry, you go," she said.

Jack swallowed, and caught Melanie's eye across the table. "I was only going to say that—"

Whatever he was about to say was lost amid a deafening crash overhead. Seconds later, shards of glass rained down from the broken cupula as something heavy fell through the air, landing on the table directly in front of Anna and Frank, splintering the wood with a sickly *crunch*.

It was the body of a young woman.

CHAPTER 3

Somebody was screaming, Anna thought, before realising belatedly that the sound was coming from her own lips. The dead woman's face stared unseeingly at her from bloodshot eyes, her neck twisted at an unnatural angle to the rest of her broken body. The force of the fall had cracked the table and sent the crockery and candelabra flying, scattering towards the diners who raised their arms instinctively to prevent injury. They couldn't stop the fall of glass, pieces of which sliced their skin and, in Anna's case, lodged painfully in her left shoulder blade, which was bare in the strappy red evening gown she wore.

Pain spread along her nerve endings, burning like fire.

"Are y'alreet, pet?" Frank asked, having already been assured that Denise was unharmed.

"I—it's my shoulder."

He made a quick inspection, and saw an angry chunk of glass wedged in her pale skin, which seeped a thin trail of blood down her back.

"Aye, there's a bit of a scratch there," he said, then looked across at the staring, dead eyes of the corpse lying in front of them and was reminded that he'd seen worse things in his time.

"It's bad, then," Anna said, breathing hard against waves of pain. "You're a terrible liar, Frank."

He gave her a rueful smile and raised a hand to Ryan, who was racing around the table towards them, having already checked that both Mel and the Chief Constable were unharmed.

"Jack! Charlie! Get onto the roof!" he barked, as he passed them on the way. "I want to know if anyone's still up there!"

Both detectives drew back their chairs and raced towards the staircase, taking the steps two at a time. Without knowing how the unfortunate woman had come to fall through the glass cupula, there was a chance she might have been pushed, and that the perpetrator was still there.

Satisfied that Pinter had taken command of the body, and Faulkner was already ushering people away from the crime scene and into a nearby drawing room with the help of the estate staff, Ryan turned to his wife, who looked pale and shaken.

"Anna," he breathed, and took her hands in his gentle grip. "Are you hurt?"

"It's her back, lad," Frank said, as calmly as he could, while Anna began to tremble in shock.

Ryan glanced at the injury, saw the jagged edge of a sizeable piece of glass protruding from her skin, and his jaw tightened.

"Should we take it out?" Frank wondered aloud.

"No," Ryan said, in a matter-of-fact tone which did a reasonably good job of hiding his own fear. "It's like a knife injury; if you remove it, the wound will bleed more. At the moment, the glass is stemming the flow, so it should stay there for now. I need to take Anna to Accident and Emergency as soon as possible—"

"I f-feel cold," she whispered.

Without a word, Ryan shrugged out of his dinner jacket, and, given the location of her injury, fed her arms through the sleeves so that it hung at the front rather than over her back.

"If you stay with her, Frank, I'll bring the car around—"

"I've called an ambulance, the paramedics are on their way," Denise interrupted them, taking stock of the situation in one all-encompassing glance. "There are a few others with injuries that need tending, so it makes sense to transport everyone together. Anna? Let's move you to somewhere more comfortable, darlin'."

Her soft Irish burr was never more comforting.

"Oh, my goodness!" Barbara, the events manager, hurried over to see them. "I—I can't believe it...this is awful. What can I do?"

"Do you have a quiet space?" Ryan asked her.

"Yes, yes of course, this way—"

"Ryan, you should manage things here," Denise said, in an undertone. "Just because they're a roomful of police staff, doesn't mean they aren't prone to histrionics. Most of them have never seen a dead body, before, and the same goes for the estate staff."

Ryan was still unwilling to leave his wife.

"We'll take care of her, lad," Frank said, and put a reassuring hand on his shoulder.

There were few people Ryan would ever trust to look after Anna as well as he could, but Frank and Denise were more than friends; they were *family*.

Just then, there came the delectable sound of one of the support staff emptying their stomach on the floor, the sight of violent death and spilled brain matter not mixing well with the turkey and roast potatoes they'd just consumed.

Ryan swore softly, then nodded. "My mother's at home, babysitting Emma," he said. "Could you—"

"I'll call her," Denise said.

"I'll be fine," Anna said, and managed a watery smile. "I'm sure it isn't as bad as it looks."

Ryan knew that was all bravado, but he also knew that somebody needed to take charge of a scene that was liable to turn into chaos, before long.

"I'll be as fast as I can," he promised, and brushed Anna's lips with his own.

"I blame you for this," she said weakly, as they lowered her onto a comfortable armchair set out in the library. "I *knew* you'd tempted Fate."

"Southerners," Phillips put in, with a wink.

Ryan stepped back into the atrium, took a quick survey of the damage, then moved directly towards the Chief Constable, who was helping one of the estate staff bandage a shallow cut to their arm.

"How bad?" he asked.

"Superficial, thankfully," Sandra said, and smiled at the woman, who turned out to be called Lesley. "Still worth having the paramedics look it over, when they arrive."

Lesley thanked her and moved off towards the library, which had become an unofficial field hospital for the wounded.

"How's Anna?"

"It's a bad cut, so she'll need stitches," he said. "Aside from that, she should be fine. Hopefully, there isn't any damage to the nerves in her back. What do we know about this woman?"

They looked at the young woman who lay prostrate on the tabletop. She was somewhere in her mid to late twenties, with dark curly hair and the kind of medium-toned skin that spoke of Mediterranean heritage. Pinter was performing a careful assessment, his nimble hands inspecting her for clues while Faulkner snapped pictures.

"Her name's Kimberley Foster," Sandra said, quietly. "She's already been identified by one of the estate staff."

"Which one?"

"He introduced himself as 'Adrian'," she replied, and scanned the room until she spotted him standing with a few of his colleagues. "Apparently, he takes care of all sorts around the estate, anything from maintaining and winding the clocks, to oiling hinges, joinery, and whatnot. You name it, he does it."

"Sounds like a useful man to have around," Ryan remarked, following her line of sight. "How does he know the deceased?"

"She was a conservator, cataloguing some of the old collections on the estate," she replied. "He knows all of the staff who work here, so he tells me."

Ryan spotted Mel approaching, and signalled her over. "Are you okay?" he asked.

She touched a hand to her cheekbone, which displayed a long scratch, but nodded. "No serious damage," she confirmed. "What can I do, boss?"

"There's one long driveway in and out of the estate," he said. "It's the main access. With the exception of the ambulance service, I don't want any vehicles coming or going until we have a clearer idea of what happened. I need to know—"

"Vehicle plates in the car park and the staff car park," she finished for him, already having thought ahead. "I'll take a video of them on my phone—it'll be faster."

"Good thinking," he said. "I need all the staff—including catering—rounded up. They won't like it, but nobody can leave yet."

"I'll take care of that," Morrison offered.

Ryan watched them leave, then went in search of Tom Faulkner, who stood beside Jeff Pinter taking photographs of the crime scene on his mobile phone to capture any small details that may later prove to be important.

"I need a couple of clear plastic sandwich bags," Pinter was saying.

"Now isn't the time to think about a doggy bag, Jeff." Ryan surveyed the remains of what had once been an attractive young woman.

"Har har," Pinter replied, archly. "I need to protect her hands, in case there's any trace evidence."

"I'll ask the catering staff if they have any," Faulkner volunteered, and went off in search of makeshift evidence bags.

"Well?" Ryan said. "Any preliminary thoughts?"

Pinter sighed deeply, and wished he hadn't had quite so many glasses of fizz. Of all the people in the room, he was usually the one most able to deal with the hard face of death, given that was his chosen profession. However, that didn't factor in the alcohol and rich food currently swirling around his gut and making a mockery of his years of practical experience.

"As you can see, she landed face down on the table, which tends to indicate a push as opposed to a fall, purely as a matter of probability," he began. "You know as well as I do that, in cases where someone has pushed another person, they usually do it while their victim's back is turned and with considerable force. That means the victim tends to land on their front, and falls quite quickly." He paused, cocking his head to one side, considering the blunt force trauma to the girl's head. Then, he reached across and, with hands protected by a pair of rubber gloves provided by the estate staff, he gently lifted one of the girl's arms to inspect them for damage.

"I can't see any obvious defensive wounds on her forearms, which you might expect to see if a person was holding off an attack," he said. "That being said, defensive marks aren't always immediately apparent. Contrary to popular belief, bruises often take a few days to develop on a body, which is why I usually take a second look a few days after my initial postmortem before writing a final report. Otherwise, it's easy to form a conclusion without having seen everything the body has to tell us."

Pinter could be a fastidious man, prone to idiosyncrasies that were often irritating, but Ryan would never say that he was anything other than a leader in his field, and a loyal member of the constabulary's team. Over the years he'd known him, Pinter's professional opinion had often played a crucial part in solving a murder enquiry. If he said it was important to exercise patience then, no matter how frustrating, that's what they'd do.

"Without firm DNA evidence, or any other injuries, the question of how someone came to fall often comes down to an assessment of situational factors," Pinter added.

Ryan agreed, which was why he would be instructing Faulkner and his team of forensics staff to perform a thorough search of the roof around the broken cupula window, as well as the access points surrounding it, to find any minutiae that might indicate a struggle—scuff marks, fragments of clothing, skin samples and anything else that could help them to build a picture of whether Kimberley fought off an aggressor, or fell through the glass without any additional help. In the coming days, they'd question her family, her friends and colleagues, and any romantic partners to gain a better understanding of the person she'd been. Crucially, they needed to know whether she had any reason to take her own life or, alternatively, if there was any reason somebody else might have wanted to take it from her.

"Faulkner might want to do a reconstruction, before the cupula window is repaired," Ryan said, thinking of other times when the forensics team had used digital simulations and even weighted models to test the dynamics of the fall site, assessing the angles and speed necessary to bring about an impact such as the one Kimberley had suffered.

Pinter nodded, and leaned forward to study one of her hands, checking again to see if there was anything visible to the naked eye.

"You're sure the fall killed her?" Ryan said. "What if she was already dead on impact?"

Pinter shook his head and pointed towards a pool of blood near the woman's head, which had soaked into her hair so that it was now a congealed, muddy reddish-brown colour.

"There wouldn't be anywhere near that volume of blood, if she was already dead," he said. "The heart stops pumping it around the body."

Ryan nodded, and was about to ask another question when he heard his name being called. He looked up to see Jack hanging over the gallery rail on the first floor, waving him up.

He left the pathologist to his ministrations, and flew upstairs.

CHAPTER 4

Ryan found Jack and Charlie waiting for him at the top of the stairs.

"We've cleared the first floor," Jack told him. "We've searched everywhere for an access route to the attic level, and this is the only door left to try, but it's locked." He pointed to an old wooden doorway, directly at the head of the stairs.

"We've tried forcing it, but it won't budge," Charlie said.

Ryan gave the door another tug, for good measure, but had to agree that whoever had built the hall had certainly built it to last. "You're sure there isn't any other access?"

"Nothing obvious," Jack replied. "We need to get this door open."

Ryan thought of Adrian, who'd been billed as a one-stop-shop for all useful jobs, big and small, then leaned over the gallery rail to scan the remaining crowd. "*Adrian*!"

The estate officer had the weathered face of a man who'd enjoyed spending time outdoors, offset by the quiet demeanour of one who also enjoyed tinkering with clocks and fixing cars. He looked up in surprise at the sound of his name, and moved to the base of the stairs to call back. "Aye? Can I help you?"

"We need access to the roof, so we can check the broken window," Ryan called back. "Is there a key to unlock this door at the top of the stairs?"

"You can only open that door from the other side," Adrian explained. "You get to the other side through a servant's entrance door outside, or inside, through the kitchens. Best if I run around to the side entrance and let you in, it'll be quicker that way."

Ryan thanked him, and they waited what seemed like long minutes until they heard the turn of a key in the lock on the other side of the oak panelled door. It swung open to reveal Adrian silhouetted in the dim light of the hallway beyond, and he stepped back so they could cross the threshold. As they did so, they were struck by the distinct feeling of having left one world for another. On the other side of the door, there were no fine furnishings, no paintings or ornate architecture; this was the servants' domain, where bare floorboards and unpretentious, whitewashed walls prevailed. A set of rickety back stairs led down to the kitchens and cellars, and upward to the attic rooms. Multiple doors led into storage rooms and other multi-purpose areas that had been used by the military as officers' quarters, tuck shop and mess during the Second World War, so they would later discover. The whole area was covered in a fine film of dust and cobwebs, which told them the place was no longer in constant use.

"Which way to the roof?" Charlie asked.

"Up the back stairs to the next floor," Adrian told them. "I can show you, if you like?"

Ryan turned to Jack and Charlie. "I'll check out the roof, while the two of you sweep the top floor attic rooms," he said, then turned back to Adrian. "Was the external door locked, by the way?"

"It was locked," he confirmed. "I opened it with my own set of keys."

Ryan nodded. "All right, let's go."

The four of them hurried to the back stairs and climbed one flight up to the attic floor, which was in darkness.

"Careful as you go; the lights can be a bit unreliable, up here," Adrian explained. "The system needs re-wiring, which we're hoping to convince the new owner to pay for. Hopefully it'll hold out—"

He reached for an old switch, which looked as aged as the house, and a series of strip lights flickered on, casting an eerie, energy-saving glow along the long attic corridor.

They paired off, and went in search of answers.

Jack and Charlie walked shoulder-to-shoulder along the attic corridor, which followed the perimeter of the central atrium. Owing to the shape of the roof, the attic floor appeared invisible from the outside of the hall, which, at first glance, only appeared to have two floors rather than three. It seemed a fitting metaphor, Charlie thought, for the role of servants at the time the hall had been built; namely that, like the third floor, they should be inconspicuous. A number of doors led off the corridor, and they paused to open each one and check inside as they passed, exercising caution in case somebody was indeed loitering in one of the dusty old rooms.

"These must have been the servants' bedrooms, at one time," Charlie said, as they stepped inside another one that was a mirror image of the last, with the same faded, peeling wallpaper, bare floors and small cast iron fireplace which would, at one time, have afforded much-needed heat during the bitterly cold winter months. Now, the grates were empty, and there was a chill on the air, helped along in no small part by the single-paned sash windows that rattled in the wind.

"There are so many of these rooms," Jack replied, in hushed tones, as if to raise his voice would also raise the ghosts of a hundred servants.

"It's a big place," she said. "In its hey-day, the Edgington family would've kept a huge staff to cater to their every need."

"How the other half live," he said, good-naturedly. "Mind you, I couldn't stand to have people roaming around my house all the time. What if I fancied walking around naked one Tuesday afternoon, and the old butler wandered in to find me in my birthday suit?"

He was only joking, Charlie thought, and yet she was glad of the poor lighting to hide the tell-tale flush rising up her throat at the very mention of Jack in the nude.

Get a grip, she told herself.

Not *that* kind of grip, she added, swiftly.

"Shall we move onto the next one?"

"Mm hm," she said.

They visited the next room, and the one after that. Each of the small bedrooms had a sash window overlooking the central cupula, through which they could see Ryan stepping out onto the flat, leaded roof surrounding it, nothing more than a shadow moving in the darkness.

"It might have been an accident," Jack said, as they turned away from the window. "It's windy out there and, if somebody was having a fag or a vape, it would be easy for them to trip and lose their balance—"

Whatever he'd been about to say was snatched from his lips, when suddenly the lights cut out and they were plunged into darkness.

To his eternal shame, Jack squealed, and made a grab for Charlie's hand.

She should have let it go and stepped away, she thought.

But she did neither.

"I didn't know you were afraid of the dark," she said, softly.

"I'm not," Jack replied, and she felt his warm breath against her face, smelling faintly of nut roast. "It's things that *hide* in the dark that I'm afraid of. Haven't you ever seen a horror movie? The killer always jumps out of a closet when the lights go out, or the hero runs into a giant cobweb when they're trying to make a getaway—"

"You're afraid of spiders, too?" she said, sweetly.

"*No*," he lied. "I just don't like things that move faster than I do."

"I can run faster than you. Does that mean you don't like me?"

Jack was momentarily lost for words and, as the darkness wrapped itself around them like a cocoon, he felt himself lean towards her, his body reaching out to hers.

There was a short, charged silence, and then she let go of his hand.

"Come on," she said. "Let's use the torches on our phones, the light'll scare off any creepy crawlies."

She stepped away, and he had no choice but to follow.

"There's nobody up here."

Having instructed Adrian to remain in the corridor, Ryan searched the roof around the broken cupula, which consisted of a flat walkway upon which it was possible to sit and smoke, or perhaps chat with a friend during a lunch break. The main roof rose up at a higher level on all sides, blocking the view of the wider countryside and creating a kind of rooftop courtyard, with the broken window in the centre.

"Could've been a nasty accident, if she came out here to look at the stars and lost her balance," Adrian called out to him. "It's tragic, but that's exactly why we tell people to be careful."

Ryan said nothing, but continued to search the area using his phone torch for light, crouching to snap pictures of the area around the entrance, which was a heavy metal door that required another key to open it.

"Who has a key to this door, aside from you?" he asked.

Adrian thought about it.

"Almost all the full-time estate staff, although there's also a copy in the key safe in the estate office," he said, which didn't narrow things down over-much, Ryan thought sourly.

"What about other access points?" he said, as a gust of icy wind whipped around them and whistled through the fragments of cupula still hanging from its frame. "Can you get up here any other way besides the back stairs?"

Adrian shook his head.

"They're the only stairs up to the attic level," he said, and then thought for a moment. "You can get through the door we used at the top of the main stairs, but you'd need somebody to open it for you on the other side, just as I did to let you in. Otherwise, there's the servant's door which leads straight onto the carriage driveway, outside. On the ground floor, you can go through the old kitchens to find your way back into the main part of the house, but it takes longer, and you'd have to go through the working part of the house where any one of the staff might see you."

"You're thinking like a detective," Ryan said, eyeing the man closely.

Adrian looked mildly embarrassed. "Just tryin' to put myself in the mind of someone out to do no good," he said. "Those are the only ways in or out, anyhow."

Ryan nodded. "I appreciate the help," he said.

Before he could utter another word, the lights went out in the corridor behind Adrian, though a quick glance at the broken window told them they were still operational in the atrium below.

"Damn," Adrian muttered. "The fuse must've tripped again. I can fiddle with it and try to get the lights back on, so your colleagues don't take a tumble—the floor's a bit uneven and there's junk in some of the rooms."

"I thought the conservation work took place on this level of the house?" Ryan said, as he stepped back through the metal door and into the corridor, which was only mildly warmer than outside.

"Aye, but they're still sortin' through all the paraphernalia," Adrian explained. "The hall was used as a military base during the Second World War, and the soldiers left all sorts behind when they decamped. They moved around a lot of family memorabilia, so it's been a job and a half to put it all back into good order."

"I understand the dead woman was a conservator," Ryan prodded. "Did you know her?"

Was it a trick of his torch light, Ryan wondered, *or did the man's face become shuttered?*

"I knew her in passing, aye," Adrian said. He made a kind of tutting sound in the back of his throat, and then took himself off to find the fuse box, leaving Ryan to ponder the old saying about it always being the quiet ones you had to watch.

CHAPTER 5

"This door is locked." Charlie twisted the old door knob this way and that, but it wouldn't budge.

"Let's have a look?"

"Be my guest." She stood aside to allow Jack to move forward, shivering slightly in the thin material of her evening dress so the light from her phone torch bobbed up and down.

Jack swore softly, set down his own torch light, and began shrugging out of his dinner jacket.

"What—what're you doing?" she demanded, a bit defensively.

"You're cold," he said. "I should have thought to do this, sooner."

"I'm fine," she argued.

"Your teeth are chattering," he shot back. "Just take the bloody jacket, will you?"

"I don't want it."

"What the hell's the matter with my jacket?" He looked down at the material he held in his hand, and thought it was a perfectly respectable rental. It might not have been bespoke tailored like Ryan's, but that was no reason for her to stick her nose up…

The torch light bobbed again, and that settled it.

"For God's sake, stop being stubborn and let me help you," he said, irritably. "Now isn't the time to be making some sort of feminist point—"

Charlie was incensed. "*Oh*, so, just because I don't want to go along with your big, macho display, that means I'm making a political point, does it? Did it ever occur to you that I don't want your second-hand sweat draped all over me?"

That cut him to the quick. "I'll have you *know*, this jacket smells like musky sandalwood, which is exactly what was promised by that expensive aftershave I bought from the *Fenwick's* counter, last week," he snapped, referring to a famous old department store in the middle of Newcastle.

"You were robbed!" she threw back, all her romantic frustrations pouring out alongside the fear that lay beneath them. She'd made herself vulnerable once before and been burned, badly. After promising herself she'd never be vulnerable like that again, she'd forgotten her own good advice the moment she'd met Jack, and had begun to soften, unfurling like a flower in spring, only to be disappointed again. She couldn't wear his clothing, Charlie thought, because it would smell of him, and torment her all the more.

In answer, he took matters into his own hands and draped the jacket around her shoulders. "Deal with it," he said, flatly. "The last thing we need is you coming down with hypothermia in that skimpy dress."

"It's *not* skimpy! It's an evening gown, not that I'd expect you to know the difference!"

"Oh really? Then, why does it cling so much to—to—everything," he finished, lamely, thinking of the way the deep ochre-coloured silk skimmed her body and clung to its curves like a second skin.

The fight drained out of him, suddenly.

"It's a beautiful gown," he said softly, and the atmosphere became electric again. "I'm sorry, I was only trying to help because you're cold."

"I know," she said, almost inaudibly. "Thank you."

"You're welcome."

Charlie held her breath as they looked at one another through the shadows.

"Let's try the next door," Jack said, and stepped away.

They followed the corridor around a corner, tracing the perimeter of the hall, and found the next three doors to be locked.

"These must be the conservation rooms, where the archive collections are being stored," Charlie ventured, as they continued to move carefully through the darkness. "They're probably locked, for security reasons."

"Archive collections?"

"Yes, I was chatting to one of the estate staff—Michelle, I think? She was telling me there's a small team who've been appointed by the family trust to catalogue and care for all the artefacts. There's so much room up here, apparently they decided it was the perfect place to keep everything and get a bit of peace and quiet from visitors tramping around during the day."

"If the dead woman was one of the team, what was she doing up here at night?" Jack wondered aloud. "Surely, there's no call for her to be working on a weekend, in the evening *and* at Christmastime?"

"The odds are looking less likely for an accidental death," Charlie had to say.

They continued onward, their footsteps sounding impossibly loud as the floorboards protested beneath them, until they came to a door that wasn't locked.

In fact, it stood ajar.

"Charlie—"

"I see it," she whispered. "Stand back."

"Wha—?"

She applied the heel of her elegant, stilettoed shoe to the panelled door, booting it open fully so that it swung back on its hinges.

Jack goggled at her. "Who d'you think you are? Lara Croft?"

She snorted. "You wish."

The banter came easily—*too easily*, Charlie thought. Sparring with Jack felt so natural, their laughter a balm for the nerves and a welcome contrast to the difficult work they did, most days. In the attics of the old house, dressed in their finery and without the prying eyes of their colleagues and friends, his girlfriend—

His girlfriend, Charlie repeated silently.

Her smile faded, and she turned back to the matter in hand.

"Come on, let's go inside," she said. "If there was anybody up here with Kim, they're probably long gone by now, anyway."

But, as they entered the large, musty workroom, the thin light from their phone torches fell upon a long wall against which some industrial wooden shelves had been erected, each with different heights to accommodate a range of plaster mouldings, picture frames and other heirlooms under conservation. But it wasn't the pictures or the broken plasterwork that quickened their hearts. It was the collection of long canvas shrouds covering what, at first glance, appeared to be three or four bodies lying inert—two or three on the middle rung of the large shelving unit, and another one on the floor nearby.

"Jack—" Charlie said, tremulously. "Look over there."

"I see it," he said. "Wait here, and I'll check it out."

She put a hand on his arm, and he felt the heat of it through the thin fabric of his shirt.

"We'll both check it out," she said, and stepped forward to begin searching all the nooks and crannies, shining her light behind the stacks of boxes containing what Jack might have described as 'junk' but which was, he was sure, extremely important and probably worth more than his house.

Jack watched Charlie step forward into the shadows and the thought came, unbidden, that she moved with the kind of fearless confidence he often emulated, but had never truly possessed. Oh, he'd done the occasional 'heroic' thing, but it had never been a conscious, considered choice to step outside of his comfort zone. On the other hand, Charlie was a woman who, in big and small ways, demonstrated courage every day. No matter what life threw at her, she seemed to get up each morning with renewed optimism and a spring in her step. Her consistency was the key, he realised, and it wasn't the kind of quality that could be bottled or bought. Resilience was a skill that had to be learned and, for some, the lesson came very early in life.

He set these introspections aside, and crossed the room to join her in sweeping the perimeter, peering into dark corners to be sure no evil was lurking there. Satisfied they were the only two living creatures in the room—discounting the mice that scurried behind the skirting boards, and the bats scratching in the rafters above their heads—they turned to the shrouded figures lying motionless across an entire length of sturdy wooden shelving.

Jack reached out a hand, and turned to Charlie with a questioning look. “Ready?”

She nodded. “Ready.”

He grasped the edge of the canvas and whipped it back, scattering a fine cloud of dust into the air around their heads. They both took an involuntary step back, preparing themselves for something to jump out at them—or, worse still, for the sight of an old skeleton to crumble at their feet.

In the end, neither happened.

“Is that—?” Charlie began.

“Yep,” Jack said. “That’s a bunch of old radiators.”

She pursed her lips, and continued to stare at the collection of old rusted metal. “You know, anyone might have thought there was a body beneath those dust sheets,” she said, eventually.

“Absolutely,” he agreed. “Easy mistake to make.”

They checked beneath the other sheets, just to be sure, and found more vintage articles laid out beneath. There was everything from broken plaster busts to wartime radios, none of which even remotely resembled a body.

“Well,” Charlie said, feeling mildly disappointed not to have found anything at all suspicious. “I guess that’s that.”

They stepped back into the corridor, which was still in darkness relieved only by the light from their torches.

“I’ve been thinking,” Charlie said softly.

Jack felt something leap inside his chest. “Yes?” he whispered.

"We don't have to mention this—" she began.

"To Frank? Absolutely not," he said swiftly, imagining the merciless ribbing that would surely follow if their beloved sergeant caught wind of it.

"So, the fact we managed to scare ourselves silly at the sight of some dusty old radiators stays between us?"

"Till death us do…" he started to say.

There was a short, heavy silence, where neither dared to speak. Then, unexpectedly, the lights flickered on again, and the moment was lost.

"We'd better report back to Ryan," Charlie said, and peeled his jacket from her arms before handing it back to him. "Thank you for the borrowed heat."

She turned and walked away.

CHAPTER 6

"He can pat me down any day!"

Chief Constable Morrison rolled her eyes at the bawdy laughter coming from a particular group of female estate staff, who huddled together around a large refectory table in the kitchen while discussing Ryan's personal attributes with all the restraint of a pack of ravenous lions having just spied a lone, juicy-looking wildebeest.

"I love a man in black tie," one of them was saying. "And, with his dark hair—"

She made a kind of chomping sound, and Morrison wrinkled her nose in distaste.

"And silvery blue eyes," another one chimed in.

"Don't forget his hands," one of the older ladies muttered, lasciviously. "He's got nice hands, and I'll bet he knows what to do with them, too—"

"Right! That's *it*!" Morrison burst out, with more force than she'd intended. "I've known Prince Charming for a *long* time, and I can tell you that he might look like a bloody film star, but he's human, just like the rest of us. For one thing, he's as stubborn as a mule—"

"I like a man who knows his own mind," Barbara, the Events Manager, interrupted.

Morrison folded her arms. "He can be a grumpy git, when he wants to be—" she tried again.

"Who *wouldn't* be grumpy, thinking of all the injustice in the world?" Barbara argued.

"I'm reliably informed, he has to trim his nostril hair," Morrison threw in, a bit desperately.

"Good grooming is *never* a bad thing," Barbara said, with a faraway expression on her face, and the Chief Constable realised she was fighting a battle that had already been lost. Besides, if her stalwart murder detective's pretty face provided a helpful distraction to the staff of Belsay Hall, she supposed it was no bad thing. She'd often wondered whether Ryan had any *real* idea of the impact he had on the opposite sex, and the maternal part of her hoped for his sake that he didn't, for to know the truth might have terrified him more than being alone with a serial killer in a locked room.

A few minutes later, the man himself appeared in the doorway, white dress shirt rolled up at the sleeves and bow tie loosened and tucked negligently in his pocket.

"How are things in here?" he asked.

"I think I can safely say, everyone is pretty nauseated," Morrison drawled. "How are things out there?"

"Coroner's Office are on their way to collect the body and transfer it to the mortuary," Ryan said, in an undertone. "Pinter's—"

He broke off, feeling the prickly heat of several sets of eyes boring into the back of his head. He turned around to see a group of innocent-looking women, all dressed in smart black suits and crisp white shirts. He smiled and, with unnerving synchronisation, they all beamed back at him.

"Thank you for your patience," he said. "I appreciate you must be tired and upset at what happened, this evening. If you'll bear with us a little longer, I or one of my colleagues will be with you shortly to take down a brief statement."

There were exclamations of it being no inconvenience at all, that they were happy to wait, and Ryan was impressed by their genial attitude, especially in the circumstances.

"They seem to be very cooperative," he remarked to Morrison, who raised an eyebrow and decided not to mention the small battle she'd had in trying to keep them all corralled in a single room until he'd come along.

"You must have the magic touch," she said, and, from the corner of her ear, thought she heard someone whisper, *I bet he does.*

"Pipe down!"

Ryan was taken aback. "Ma'am?"

"Not you," Morrison muttered. "I was—oh, never mind. Has the ambulance arrived?"

"Yes, the paramedics are with the injured in the library, right now," he said. "Pinter's done all he can from here, and Faulkner's photographed everything he can think of, too. He's taken himself off to walk around the perimeter of the house and check for access points or footprints."

"Good thinking," Morrison murmured, and Ryan nodded.

"What about the roof?" she asked.

Ryan moved further away from prying ears before answering. "It's next on Faulkner's list—he's waiting for the rest of his team to arrive, and he'll make a start on sweeping the area for any traces," he replied. "I had a quick look up there, but there was nothing untoward; I couldn't see any personal effects left behind, and there were no obvious signs of a struggle. If it weren't for the circumstances of her fall, and the timing, I'd have been inclined to say it was an accident."

They both fell silent for a moment, considering the prospect.

"As you say, the timing is strange, no matter which way you look at it," Morrison said. "It's highly unlikely that she'd need to be on site for work at this time of night, and considering it's the weekend, which calls into question whether she took herself up there to meet someone or for another reason."

"Suicide, you think?" Ryan murmured, beneath his breath. "We'll have a clearer idea of her mental state, once we've spoken to her colleagues, friends and family."

Morrison nodded. "Even if there was a reason for her to want to take her own life, why choose an evening when the Hall would be occupied, and in such an ostentatious way? Usually, people go somewhere quiet, where they'll be alone."

Ryan agreed. "There's more to this than meets the eye," he decided. "Whatever that is, we'll find it."

Morrison thought to herself that, one of the things she *hadn't* told Ryan's Unofficial Fan Club was that he was an outstanding detective, who simply never gave up. His tenacity was the stuff of legend, and his moral yardstick unimpeachable. A Chief Constable could tolerate the occasional bad mood, if that was the trade-off.

She smiled at him. "I know you will," she said. "You always do."

He left a moment later, leaving a cloud of pheromones behind him, and Morrison turned to the remaining crowd of staff. Barbara opened her mouth, as if to say something else, but she was forestalled by a single, frosty look from the Chief.

"I'm warning you," she said. "The very next person to utter a *single flattering comment* about DCI Ryan is going to find themselves in handcuffs—"

"I wouldn't say 'no'," one of them giggled, and the whole room exploded.

"Reprobates," she said to herself, and flopped down into the nearest chair.

CHAPTER 7

As the bell in the clock tower chimed midnight, Ryan and his team gave permission for police and estate staff to return to their homes, having taken down their preliminary statements while the events of the evening were still fresh in their minds. Jeff Pinter accompanied Kimberley Foster's body back to the mortuary in Newcastle, ahead of a postmortem examination he would conduct the following day—probably with the assistance of several painkillers to combat the brutal hangover that was sure to follow. Faulkner's team of forensic examiners were still scouring an area far larger than the average scene, and would not be returning home for several hours yet. To help with their task, large, industrial lights had been set up on the roof, which was afforded some protection from the elements by the hasty erection of a large tarpaulin tent, which billowed as the wind continued to rush up and over the eaves and swirl around the flat, inner roof where the glass atrium window had once been.

As the tail-lights of the coroner's van disappeared down the long driveway, Ryan made his way back through the atrium and into the library, which was no longer a field hospital but a meeting place for his weary team, who congregated on a collection of pintucked leather sofas arranged around a large fireplace that bore the dying embers of a fire in its grate. Anna was the only addition to the police crowd, her wound having been cleaned and bandaged by paramedics and pronounced shallow enough to avoid the need for stitches, after all.

Ryan crossed the room and perched on the broad arm of the sofa beside her, one foot planted on the floor while the other swung negligently beside it. "Almost time to go home," he murmured.

"Take as long as you need," Anna said, and then stifled a yawn.

He smiled, and leaned down to brush his lips over the top of her hair before turning to the others. His team resembled a bunch of characters from an old murder mystery film, he thought, all dressed in evening wear, the dying firelight casting shadows over their faces so they appeared to be different versions of the people he knew so well. Wooden panelling surrounded them on all sides, half-filled with old books yellowed with age, and the wind whistled through tiny gaps in the sash windows and whipped down the chimney, howling like a person in torment.

They all shivered, though the room was warm enough.

"One of the staff was telling me this place is haunted," Mel said, breaking the silence. "Apparently, if you go into one of the rooms upstairs, or in certain parts of the garden, you feel a chill. Some people claim to have seen a beautiful, dark-haired woman walking around, holding a candle."

There was a pause, and then Frank wriggled his fingers and said—

"*Woooooooooooooooh*!"

Denise gave him a playful jab in the ribs. "All of these old places seem to be haunted," she said, easily. "It's good for business."

"There'll be another ghost, after tonight," Morrison said, and brought them all back to reality with a thud. "What do you reckon, Ryan? Is the death of Kimberley Foster suspicious or not?"

He considered all that they knew so far, which wasn't much. They had a young woman who'd hurtled to her death, though every statement given by estate staff was unanimous in saying she'd been a bubbly, cheerful sort of person, without any suggestion of depressive illness. They'd need to confirm that by looking at her medical history and by speaking with her family—whom he'd had the sad task of calling, earlier in the evening to convey the terrible news. Until more information could be gathered, he couldn't say with confidence that her death was entirely benign, which left him only one option, as the Senior Investigating Officer.

"Suspicious," he pronounced. "Aside from everything else, there's a ledge separating the cupula window from the rest of the flat roof surrounding it, which acts as a kind of barrier. It would have taken extreme bad luck, or extreme force, for anyone to have fallen over it with enough velocity to smash through the glass."

There were nods around the room, then Frank heaved a dramatic sigh.

"What now?" Morrison exclaimed.

He shrugged, and then folded his hands across his paunch, which was sheathed beneath a smart white shirt with seventies-style ruffles running down the front. "I *told* you we should have stuck with a pie and a pint, down the pub, didn't I?" he said, a bit smugly. "For one thing, we've never had any cadavers droppin' in our gravy, and, for another, we always had time for a round of karaoke—"

"I'll keep it in mind," she interjected, with surly humour. "Now, bugger off, the lot of you—and Merry Christmas!"

Anna had fallen asleep in the backseat of their taxi by the time the driver brought it to a stop outside their new home in the picturesque coastal village of Bamburgh. As the engine fell silent, Ryan looked across at his wife, peaceful and beautiful in the moonlight, her face only slightly paler than usual as a result of the pain in her shoulder. Her hair had grown back since being forced to cut it short, and it fell in shining dark waves over her shoulders, reminding him of how she'd looked when they first met.

"Here you go," he said, handing the driver a wad of cash with a generous tip included. "Thanks for keeping the journey smooth."

"No bother, mate," came the reply. "You need a hand with anythin'?"

Ryan shook his head. "I've got this," he said quietly, and unfolded himself from the car. Then, he walked around to open Anna's door, and reached inside to undo her seatbelt.

Her eyelids fluttered open at the shock of cool air, which carried a faint scent of the sea. "Are we home?"

"Yes," he said. "Take my hand, and I'll help you out of the car."

Anna forgot about her shoulder, and started to haul herself from the car, only to fall back again with a sharp cry of pain that brought tears to her eyes.

"Careful, my love," he murmured. "Take it easy."

Feeling more tired than she could ever remember, Anna nodded, and Ryan supported her as she stepped out. Then, with deft and gentle hands, he swung her up into his arms.

"Rest against me," he said. "Those pills have wiped you out."

The emergency doctor who'd accompanied the paramedics had prescribed a couple of extra strength painkillers, which had alleviated the pain for a while, as well as making her feel as though she was floating on air.

"I do feel a bit woozy," she admitted, and gave him a big, silly smile. Her head fell against his chest as they approached the front door, which his mother held open in readiness for them.

"How is she?" Eve mouthed.

"Tired and sore," Ryan replied. "It'll hurt in the morning."

"Let's get her to bed, then," his mother said, with a loving smile for the woman she considered a daughter. "I'll help to get her ready, if you like?"

Ryan thanked her, and they made their way inside the old house they'd recently bought, and were in the midst of renovating. It had once belonged to a local philanthropist by the name of Angela Bansbury—no connection to *Lansbury*—whose murder they'd investigated a while back. She'd left the old Georgian house to her longtime gardener, in gratitude for his kindness over so many years, and he'd chosen to sell it to a new family who could breathe life into its old walls and make new memories in that lovely house overlooking the sea. As for their old house in Elsdon…

It had been a wrench to leave the home they'd built together, but they could no longer continue living in a place marred by the death of his father, Charles Ryan.

It was just too painful.

And so, they'd come to the same decision as Angela's gardener. Namely, that it was high time for a new family to enjoy their beautiful home on the hill overlooking Elsdon, and wake up to birdsong in the mornings.

Luckily, they knew the perfect family.

Frank and Denise paid off their taxi and made their way across a smart gravel driveway towards the front door of their new home, which had been acquired from Ryan and Anna for a suspiciously low asking price, which, Ryan had insisted, was the maximum amount they would *ever* accept from their nearest and dearest friends. There had been much back-and-forth on the subject, some vague and insincere threats of violence from Frank if Ryan wouldn't at least accept a bit more for the place but, ultimately, the younger man had won that particular battle. Help had come from Samantha, who reminded her mother and father of how convenient it would be to live right next to the stables where her horse, Pegasus, was liveried. The horse had been her only friend in the world, when Frank and Denise had adopted Sam, and girl and beast remained inseparable.

"Alreet, put it there," Frank had capitulated, offering his hand to Ryan with a grateful smile before adding quietly, "I won't forget this. You've made our dream a reality."

Ryan had smiled, and given his friend a clap on the back. "You're getting soft, in your old age," he'd replied, and proceeded to ask whether Frank had completed a dementia check, lately.

Naturally, this led to further mild and insincere threats of violence.

Now, as they entered the hallway of their beautiful new home, Frank and Denise paused to savour their surroundings.

"I'd be happy anywhere with you, pet," he said, slipping an arm around his wife's waist. "All the same, I could get used to all this fresh air and wide-open space. I quite fancy myself as a country gent, y'nah."

"I'll tell you a secret," Denise replied, and turned to clasp his loveable face between her hands. "I could quite fancy you as a country gent as well."

With that, she planted a smacking kiss against his upturned mouth.

"*Whey*, you should have said sooner," he declared, once he got his breath back. "I've got a nice little tweed number in the wardrobe, and I'm sure I've got a flat cap knockin' about here somewhere—"

"I said a 'country gent', not an extra from *Peaky Blinders,*" she laughed.

"Not much difference between them, if you ask me," he quipped.

"You might be right," she chuckled, and slipped off her shoes. "Oh, Jesus, Mary and Joseph…that feels better. My feet were killing me."

"I'll give them a rub, if you like?"

Just for that, she gave him another kiss. "You're one in a million, Frank," she declared, and made her way through to the living room, where they found the remains of a pizza sitting on the coffee table beside a half-drunk bottle of lemonade and some empty sweet wrappers.

"Doesn't take a detective to figure out who was here before us," he said, and made her laugh again. "That lass of ours is turnin' into a right layabout—and her mate, Tallulah, is just as bad."

"They're good kids," Denise averred, and settled her feet on his lap.

They enjoyed the quiet of home for a few minutes, feeling grateful for all they had.

"Quite a night, eh?" Frank said. "I think this'll go down as one of the most memorable Christmas parties."

"Only *one* of them? I would've thought a body landing on the dining table would trump all the rest?"

Phillips rubbed her toes in a soothing, circular motion. "You never know what next year will bring," he said, and jiggled his preposterous eyebrows to make her laugh.

"How are Jack and Mel doing, d'you think?" Denise asked, changing the subject.

Frank heaved a genuine sigh. "Who knows?" he said. "The lad doesn't know whether he's comin' or goin'. First, Mel says she loves him, and they're all happy as Larry. The next thing you know, she's off to Thailand to recover from her trauma, tells him not to wait for her and to go out and find somebody else. O' course, he pines for her, and doesn't so much as look at anyone else for a good long while. Then, lo and behold, Charlie happens along, and shows him the possibilities. Just as Jack's startin' to imagine movin' on, Mel comes back and tells him she still loves him." He blew out a gusty breath. "Like I say, he doesn't know his arse from his elbow, at the moment."

Denise made a murmuring sound of agreement. "I feel for Charlie," she said. "I like Mel, very much, and always have, but…"

"Aye," Frank agreed, without her having to say it. "I know what you mean. But there's nothin' fair in love and war. Sometimes, the timin' just isn't right."

Denise thought of a time when Frank had been married to his first wife, Laura, who'd been diagnosed with terminal cancer in her late forties. He'd nursed her, eventually taking time off work to be with her all the time, with a tenderness that couldn't fail to inspire. Denise had never, by word or deed, breathed a word of her feelings for him until long after Laura's passing, and only when she was fairly sure the news would be welcomed.

"Timing is everything," she agreed.

"Which one d'you think he'll choose?" Frank asked, after another minute of sitting in comfortable silence.

Denise shook her head. "If I'm not mistaken, Charlie has removed herself from the playing field," she said. "She knows what every woman knows, in their heart."

He looked up, with interest. "What's that?"

Denise closed her eyes, and rested her head back against the pillow. "You can't force anyone to love you," she said. "Feelings have to be given freely, not coerced because of circumstance or trickery. If Jack were to come to her now, and tell her he cared for her while he's still with Mel, Charlie knows she could never trust him—not really."

Frank nodded slowly. "Aye, it's true," he said. "Besides, wantin' someone isn't the same as lovin' them."

She opened her eyes, and smiled at him. "It's best when they come together," she said.

"Aye," he said, and tugged her onto his knee. "Now, does this dress count as a bit of feminine trickery? Because I want you to know, I don't mind bein' coerced into bed, if that's the case."

"Give over!" she said, and slapped at his wandering hands. "I don't need any special tricks for you, Frank Phillips; I've only got to look at you funny, and you're chasin' me up the stairs—"

"You gave me a funny look, just then," he growled, and made a playful lunge for her.

"That's just your eyesight getting worse," she managed.

"Same difference."

"You were quiet on the journey home." Mel draped her woollen coat on the back of a chair in the living room, and turned to face him.

"Was I?" Jack said, evasively. "I didn't realise."

Mel watched him walk across the open plan living space towards the kitchen area, where he reached for a glass.

"Would you like some water?" he asked, without looking at her.

"No, thanks," she said quietly. "Jack…is everything alright?"

His hand stilled on the tap. "Why wouldn't it be?"

Melanie ran an agitated hand through her hair, then padded across the floor to join him in the kitchen. "I thought you'd be happy that I came back," she said.

Jack inhaled sharply. "I am," he said, but wondered if that was the whole truth. "I'm happy you're feeling well enough to come home, in the first place."

"That isn't the same thing," she said.

"I don't know what you want me to say," he said, irritably. "You left, after telling me not to hold any candles for you. You barely reply to any of my messages—which I sent almost *daily*—and then, one day, you decide to turn up again, as if nothing had happened."

"I wanted to surprise you," she whispered.

It was certainly a surprise, he thought.

"I still love you," she said, and walked around the kitchen island to slip her arms around his waist. "Do you—Jack, do you still love me, too?"

"Of course, I love you," he said. "I've been sitting here, in this house, every night, worrying about you for months. I didn't know where you were, or how you were doing. I missed you so much."

Every word of that was true, he thought. Yet, there were different kinds of love, and he wondered whether the love he felt for her burned as brightly as it once had.

You know the answer to that, his heart whispered.

"We're both tired," he said, and turned around to take her in his arms, comforting them both. "Let's get some sleep, and see what the morning brings."

Time, Melanie thought. *They needed time to rebuild.*

"Good idea," she said, with as much cheer as she could muster. "Are you coming?"

"I'll be along in a minute," he said.

After she'd gone, he leaned back against the countertop and scrubbed a hand over his face. As the sleeve of his jacket brushed his nose, he caught the scent of something floral.

Charlie's perfume.

He raised the cuff to his nose again, and inhaled the scent, before letting his hand fall away. He looked around the living space, his eyes passing over framed pictures of himself and Melanie in various beauty spots around the North East, then over the furniture they'd bought together over the years. There was history there, he thought, and too much love between them to be thrown away lightly.

But, when he closed his eyes that night, he dreamed of a woman with dancing brown eyes, wearing a long, silk gown the colour of the setting sun.

We could be a family, she told him.

Beside her, a little boy with messy blond hair smiled, and held out his arms.

"Daddy!" he cried.

In his sleep, Jack held him close.

CHAPTER 8

Monday

Ryan couldn't say exactly what had alerted him to the presence of a third party in the bedroom he and his wife shared, except that some sixth sense sent his eyelids flying open. Sure enough, the culprit stood inches away from where he lay, staring at him with eyes that were a mirror image of his own.

"Morning, Daddy!" His little girl leaned closer, and rubbed her button nose against his, before planting a slobbery kiss on his cheek.

"Emma," he said, and gave his young daughter a sleepy smile. "Is this your way of telling me that it's time to go downstairs for some breakfast?"

"In a minute," she said, and clambered up onto the bed, burrowing under the covers until she'd managed to appropriate a majority of the duvet cover, leaving Ryan and Anna with the extreme edges of the quilt while she spread out like a starfish in the middle of their large bed.

"Is Mummy still asleep?" she asked, in a stage whisper.

"Yes," Anna mumbled, through waves of pain emanating from the bandage on her shoulder.

"Mummy hurt her back, so you need to be careful," Ryan said.

Emma nodded, and, with infinite care, planted a kiss on her mother's hair.

"Kiss it better," she declared. "Do you need some Calpol?"

Anna smiled through the pain, and thought that she could have done with a horse tranquillizer, but she'd take whatever she could get.

"I'm going to get her some special tablets," Ryan explained. "You stay here for a moment, little one."

"I'm not little!" Emma protested. "I'm a big girl, now!"

At the grand old age of three, she was certainly bigger than she had been six months before, so they couldn't argue with the logic.

"Sorry," Ryan said, gravely. "I forgot."

Still smiling, he moved into the adjoining bathroom and rooted around for some strong painkillers. While he did that, his wife and daughter snuggled together in the bed, speaking softly.

"Did you dream about anything, sweetheart?"

Emma nodded. "There was a rocket, high up in the sky!" she said, and made an action with her little hand. "Zoom!"

Anna smiled, thinking of the space project they'd been doing at Emma's nursery. "Did you go up in the rocket?"

"Yes! I was an as—an *asonut.*"

"An astronaut?"

Emma nodded.

"That's a good word," Anna said. "Did you see the stars?"

"Uh-huh," she said. "And I saw Grandad, too."

Ryan happened to step back in, at that exact moment, and felt his heart contract. "You saw Grandad, in your dream?"

Emma nodded again. "He was with the stars," she said. "When I'm big, I'll go up in a rocket and see him."

Anna reached across to run a gentle finger over her daughter's cheek. "You don't need to go up in a rocket to see the stars," she said. "You can look up into the sky, on a clear night, and see them twinkling there."

Emma broke into a smile. "Okay!" she shouted. "I'll look at them at bedtime!"

The matter sorted, she began wriggling off the bed—but not before her mother had caught her for another kiss.

"*Mummy*!"

"Okay, you can go now," Anna said, and realised that was the only medicine she really needed. "I love you, Emma."

Ryan dropped the tablets into her hand, along with a glass of water, and gave her a slow kiss. "I'd better go and chase after her," he said.

Then, they heard the unmistakeable sound of an unsuspecting grandmother being jumped on by her granddaughter, in the spare bedroom down the hall.

"Never mind," he said, and grinned.

In the MacKenzie-Phillips household, Frank cracked open one bleary eye, then the other, and tried to remember what a good night's sleep felt like. He was sure that, at one time or another, he must have felt well rested, but it was so long ago that he'd forgotten.

"What time is it?" he muttered, to nobody in particular.

"Hfffmp," his wife replied, from her position in the bed beside him.

"That's what I thought." With considerable effort, Frank levered himself up into a seated position, then promptly fell back against the headboard with a groan.

"I thought teenagers were s'posed to sleep for longer," he complained.

"That's what I heard, too," Denise grumbled. "Did we get a genetic throwback, or something?"

"It's the bloody, blasted, buggering horse!" Frank said, without rancour. "She loves that four-legged thing so much, she's up at the crack of dawn every mornin' groomin' him, muckin' out, exercisin'—"

Denise sat up to slump against the headboard beside him.

"I suppose we can't complain about her being conscientious," she said. "Most parents struggle to get their kids out of bed in the morning, so it's a good thing for her to be motivated enough to do it herself."

"Aye, I know," Frank said, affectionately. "She's a goodun."

They both smiled, wincing only slightly at the sound of crockery clattering to the floor, somewhere in the kitchen downstairs.

"All the same—"

"Aye," Frank agreed. "Can't be too careful."

"Did you have a nice time at the Christmas party?"

Charlie's mother entered their small galley kitchen dressed in a comfortable old dressing gown, its colour faded but the material softened over time. She yawned and moved towards the kettle, setting it to boil before turning back to her daughter, who still hadn't answered.

"Well? Don't keep me in suspense!"

Charlie continued to butter the piece of toast Ben had asked for. "The meal was nice," she replied. "Until a body landed on the table."

Her mother thought she'd misheard. "Until—what?"

Charlie laughed. "I know, it sounds mad, doesn't it? But it's true. A body crashed through the atrium window and landed on the enormous dining table that was set up directly beneath it."

"Good God! Did the poor soul trip and fall?"

"We don't know yet," Charlie replied. "The investigation is still in the early stages."

Her mother nodded, and took a thoughtful sip of tea as she considered her daughter's back.

"How about before the—er—body incident? Did you see—"

"Yes," Charlie replied, a bit sharply. "I saw Jack, before you ask."

"Now, now," came the reply. "I only wondered."

"I know," Charlie sighed, and turned around to give her mother a hug, by way of apology. "But you need to remember, he has somebody else in his life, and Melanie is a nice person. They were together long before I met him."

"But I could have sworn there was something between you."

Charlie swallowed, hard. "Nothing was ever said or done to suggest that," she was forced to admit. "There might have been a—a *feeling*, but neither of us acknowledged it or acted on it."

And now it's too late, she added silently.

"It's never too late," her mother said, as though she'd spoken the words aloud. "You should tell him how you feel, Charlie."

"And humiliate myself?" she burst out. "Put him in the awful position of having to let me down? He's made his choice, Mum. Let's leave it at that."

"Charlie—"

Her daughter shook her head, and leaned in to peck her cheek. "I have to go to work, now," she said. "I'll see you later on."

"Take care, love."

"Have you seen my navy coat?"

Jack walked out of the bathroom, toothbrush in hand, and shook his head. "It might be in one of the suitcases, under the bed," he mumbled, with his mouth full of toothpaste.

"Why would it be in there?" Mel asked.

He paused to get rid of the toothbrush, and to give himself a few precious moments to formulate the correct response. "I wasn't sure when you were coming back, or even *if* you were coming back, so I washed and folded a lot of your things, in case you might need me to send them to you."

Melanie felt tears sting the back of her eyes. Not because he'd put her things out of sight, but because he'd been thoughtful enough to think of what she might have wanted, in the depths of her despair.

"Thank you," she said.

Jack gave an awkward shrug. "Do you want me to… unpack them?"

Whatever Mel might have said was interrupted by the sound of Jack's work mobile ringing loudly in the next room.

"I'd better get that," he said, and hurried through to the kitchen, where his phone lay on the counter next to the coffee machine.

"Lowerson," he said.

"It's me," Ryan said. "I've just heard from Control—some body parts have washed up near the Fish Quay, so I need you and Mel to head down there and take a look."

He nodded, and glanced over at the woman across the room. "Are you—ah—are you sure you don't need me to help out at Belsay?"

"We've got it covered," Ryan assured him, and rang off soon afterwards, leaving Jack to wonder why he felt especially disappointed at not being able to see the rest of their usual team, today.

"Everything okay?" Melanie asked, finding his expression hard to read.

"Hm? Oh, yeah, fine," he replied, with false cheer. "Ryan needs us to head down to North Shields to check out some body parts that've washed up."

"Ah, the glamour," she joked.

He smiled, but it didn't quite reach his eyes. "Don't say I never take you anywhere," he said, and held open the door for her to precede him.

CHAPTER 9

Belsay had been closed to the public pending the completion of the forensic investigation, and when Ryan pulled up to its stone-pillared gates shortly before eight-thirty, he was pleased to find a sentry guarding the main driveway logging anyone who came in or out. After a brief word of encouragement for the cold-looking young police constable, Ryan continued on through the gates and followed a long, single-track driveway that wound its way through acres of farmland, past a number of estate cottages with lights in their windows to indicate they were occupied. Ryan had obtained a full list of residents, and planned to speak with many of them later that morning to see who had the means or opportunity to be on the roof with, and potentially have pushed, Kimberley Foster the previous evening—and, more importantly, who had a *motive* to do so.

The lawns and pastures presented an Arcadian scene, with the grass still coated in a thin layer of frost, its droplets shining like diamonds in the light of the hazy morning sun. Its beauty reminded Ryan of the land surrounding Summersley, and the comparison brought with it a pang of disquiet. If he wouldn't be managing the place himself, then he needed to recruit a new estate manager—the last one having recently retired. His mother hadn't expressed any desire to manage everything herself, and was still grieving the death of his father, so there was a pressing need to find somebody—sooner, rather than later.

But that was a problem for another day.

Presently, he needed to discover what had caused a young woman to fall through a glass atrium to her death and, to do that, the matter required his full attention.

Thrusting all thoughts of Summersley from his mind, Ryan continued along the driveway until he passed the stable block with its pretty clock tower, then followed the road which circled around the back of the hall. Here, there was an open courtyard with the stables on one side, a door to the old kitchens on the other, and the back wing of the house in between. Beyond the courtyard, the driveway continued towards a parking area, passing a nearby farmhouse and a couple of cottages visible through a small cluster of trees. Wooden signs told him that it was possible to follow a pathway towards the quarry garden, or the old Mediaeval castle, which had been extended at one time to include an additional wing, before the present hall had been built to replace it.

Ryan parked his car in one of the spaces and noted a couple of other vehicles already in the car park. They included Phillips' reliable old Volvo and MacKenzie's snazzy new Jimny, which was a recent purchase in deference to their new country lifestyle, because the little four-by-four could practically climb stairs and was a valuable asset in icy weather. He didn't have the heart to tell her that, at all other times, Denise may find herself frustrated by her new car's lack of speed, comfort, agility, fuel economy or any other amenity usually coveted by the average road user.

His sergeant's vehicle was sandwiched between a vintage sports car in racing red, and a large, top-of-the-range Land Rover with a specialist metallic paint job, both of which Ryan would venture to say did *not* belong to anyone on the police payroll, unless Jeff Pinter had decided to dial up his singles game.

Aside from these, a motley assortment of smaller cars formed a neat row alongside Tom Faulkner's forensic van, which stuck out as a sore thumb and served as a reminder of why they were all there.

Death.

Tugging on a pair of ski gloves and a sturdy pair of walking boots, Ryan crunched his way across the icy gravel, eyes tracing the ground as he went. The snow had been quite deep, the previous evening, but had melted away to slush sometime during the night, so that any footprints were long gone by now. He hoped his team had managed to acquire a decent recording of how things had looked on their personal phones, but they'd all been slightly the worse for mulled wine and there was a wider margin for human error because of it.

Rounding the corner of the stables, Ryan spotted Frank standing on the far side of a turning circle in front of the hall. He was deep in conversation with Tom Faulkner, who was dressed once again in the ubiquitous garb of polypropylene suit, hair net, face mask and nitrile gloves, albeit he'd removed the latter two briefly to give himself an opportunity to breathe.

"There he is!" Phillips exclaimed, and raised a hand to wave to his friend. "Thought you must've got lost, the time it's taken you to get here!"

"Got stuck behind a tractor on the A1," he said, and the other two made understanding noises. "Did you find something on the driveway?"

They shook their heads.

"Nothing yet," Tom replied.

"Then, what are we doing standing out here in the cold?"

Frank looked at Tom, and Tom looked back at Frank.

"Bloody good question," Phillips said. "Howay, let's go back inside, before me balls drop off."

Ryan grinned at the delicate turn of phrase, and they made their way towards the main doors of the hall. Things looked different in the daylight, but the lines of the house were as imposing as ever, possibly even more so now they could be seen clearly.

"Any further forward with forensics?" Ryan asked his friend, and Tom pulled an expressive face.

"We made decent progress last night, all things considered," he replied. "I've had a team on site here since six, going over the roof around the broken window with a fine-toothed comb, but, so far, nothing of interest. We've swabbed the whole area, obviously, and Pinter will be doing the same with the girl's body, to be sure there aren't any skin cells beneath her nails or anything else to suggest she was in a fight up there on the roof." Faulkner scratched the top of his head, which was beginning to feel hot beneath the hair cap. "If it weren't for the direction of the fall, and the strange fact of her being up there in the first place, I'd think she simply suffered a dreadful accident."

"Which is what somebody might be hoping," Ryan said. "It would be convenient, wouldn't it?"

The others nodded.

"Thought we might get a better idea of what kind of person she was, if we spoke to some of her colleagues in the conservation team," Frank said. "They're all in the library, waiting to be questioned."

"Wait," Ryan said.

They froze.

"What is it?" Frank whispered. "Did you see the ghost of that woman?"

Ryan slapped a palm to his face. "No, Frank, believe it or not, I didn't see a ghost," he replied, drily. "I smell coffee nearby."

"He's right," Tom muttered. "I smell it, too."

All three raised their noses to the wind, trying to determine where the heavenly smell was coming from.

They didn't have to wait long to find out.

"Morning!" Charlie called across the atrium, boot heels clicking against the stone floor as she made her way across to them. "I don't know about you, but I needed some caffeine."

In her hands, she carried a carboard tray bearing four steaming cups of coffee which she'd begged from the kitchens.

"I knew it," Frank said, and thanked her as he reached for one of them. "As soon as we met, I thought to myself, *that lass is a goodun.*"

Charlie smiled and handed a cup to Tom, who seemed even more socially awkward than usual—which was saying something.

"Thanks," he mumbled, and took a gulp of the liquid, scalding his tongue in the process.

He started coughing, and Ryan clapped a hand against his back.

"Gan' canny," Frank advised him, with a shake of his head.

"Thanks, Charlie," Ryan said, helping himself to the last cup. "You don't have to bring us anything, you know—"

"I know," she said, and she really did know it, because Ryan hadn't tolerated any misogyny in his team, which included any expectation that the women of

Major Crimes should be responsible for washing up in the break room, or stocking up on milk and other essentials. There was a rota for these things, so it was a fair exchange for all, and there was even a small departmental budget to cover the cost—Ryan being of the idea that custard creams were a necessity for life as a murder detective.

That being said, Charlie had been brought up to show appreciation for those things you were grateful for, and that included a kind team who'd made her feel at home from the very first.

"Where's Jack…and Mel?" she asked, and hoped she sounded casual.

"They're dealing with another call-out," Ryan replied, and took a sip of his coffee while he studied her face and the emotions passing over it. "A head, a torso and somebody's left foot has washed up near the Fish Quay in North Shields, so I've sent them over to deal with it."

"It's been a while since we had any dismemberment," Frank said, conversationally, and took a sip of his coffee. "Usually, that tends to mean the killer was a pro."

Faulkner nodded. "Makes it easier to dispose of the body," he agreed. "It's more convenient to transport and bury a body in parts, or to incinerate it."

"You're a scary man to know, Tom," Charlie said, and his skin turned a shade of deep pink that brought out the freckles on his nose.

"Um…thanks," he said, dubiously. "I don't know if that's a compliment or not."

"Neither do I," Charlie laughed, and polished off the rest of her coffee. "Shall we start taking down some statements?"

"No time like the present," Ryan said, and they made their way towards the library.

Phillips hung back a moment, and gave Tom a fatherly look. "Anything you want to tell your Uncle Frank?"

"Um…not really," he replied, in confusion. "I—"

"Howay man, you can't kid a kidder! You've got the hots for that lass, or my name isn't Frank Phillips!"

Tom made a hushing motion with his hand. "Shh! For God's sake, keep your voice down!"

"Aha!" Frank said, and made an elaborate sound in the back of his throat, before saying in a highly problematic, arch-French accent, "Haw-he-haw-he-haw!"

Faulkner pinched the bridge of his nose between thumb and forefinger, to stave off a sudden headache. "Frank—"

"I know, I know, don't worry about it, mum's the word, I won't tell a soul."

Apart from Denise, he thought to himself. *That went without saying.*

"So, you gonna ask her out?"

"I don't know, Frank. I'm probably too old for her."

"Don't be daft, man, you're in the prime of life," the other man said. "Any girl'd be lucky to have you, especially since you had your hair cut and sorted out that dandruff problem—which reminds me to ask, was that a *Head & Shoulders* job?"

Tom nodded, unable to do much else.

"Aye, well, it's worked wonders," Phillips said, and took another sip of his drink while he thought of what his wife had said the previous evening about Charlie stepping back from Jack Lowerson.

If that was the case, there was no harm in anybody else asking her out to dinner, was there?

"Don't wait forever to pluck up the courage," he said. "We're none of us gettin' any younger, y'nah."

"That's a cheering thought," Tom laughed.

"Any time, lad. Any time."

CHAPTER 10

The wind was bracing as Jack and Mel made their way from his car towards the Fish Quay, in North Shields. Located on the north shore of the River Tyne and to the east of Newcastle city centre, the area had a long history dating back to the thirteenth century, when a village of shielings or fishermen's huts developed on the quay in 1225. The modern-day 'North Shields' took its name from that early development and, though much had changed in the intervening centuries, it remained a working quay with a thriving hub of local businesses where fresh fish could be bought alongside other non-fish-related enterprises. Along a promenade beside the river, cyclists and pedestrians could travel further west, towards the mouth of the river where it met the North Sea, and towards the pretty village of Tynemouth which was visible from a crop of headland known as the Spanish Battery. It was a walk that Jack and Mel had done many times before, but it was not on the cards, that day.

"I can see the local bobbies," she said, and pointed to a couple of constables in high vis, who stood at the end of a long wooden jetty guarding what looked, at first glance, to be a heap of rubbish. A small crowd of people had gathered to rubberneck, the grapevine having been in full operation that morning.

"I thought they would've put up a tent," Jack muttered. "Everyone and their gran has turned out to get an eyeful."

Mel smiled. "Human nature," she said, and cast her eyes around for one of Faulkner's team. "Forensics haven't arrived yet, by the looks of things."

"Tom's on his way," Jack said. "He rang to say he has a few things to finish up at Belsay, but he'll be along as soon as he can. They're pressed for staff, since they've had to go over such a wide area up there, and I guess a recently dead woman takes priority over a collection of body parts."

"Depends on who the body parts end up belonging to," she said.

On which note, they made their way along the wooden pier, passing underneath a canopy which offered no protection whatsoever from the biting wind rolling in from the riverside. The smell of fish was pervasive and was, they supposed, marginally better than the smell of death.

They dispatched the crowd with a few well-chosen words about causing a public nuisance, and impeding the course of an investigation, then, as the onlookers scarpered, they approached the two constables standing by.

"Thought we'd never get rid of them," the young woman said. "DC Lowerson and DC Reed, I presume?"

Jack and Mel exchanged an uncomfortable glance.

"Ah, *no*, this is DC Melanie Yates," he said. "We understand human remains were found this morning?"

The constable, whose name was Gabby Short, turned and gestured behind them, to where a heap of tarpaulin had been draped over the offending articles.

"A call came through early doors," her colleague said, in a broad Geordie accent they struggled to follow at that time of the morning. "Lad who owns the fish shop, o'er there, he rang it in. Says he spotted the head floatin' on the water, like."

"Male or female?" Mel asked.

"Hard to tell, given the state of it," Gabby replied, with a grimace. "But I'd say it was male, judging from the length of the hair and all that. Here, have a look for yourself—"

She half-turned, and Jack threw up a hand.

"Er—yeah—in just a minute," he said, swallowing bile at the very thought of what awaited them. "Any identifying features, or items found on the torso?"

"Nowt," the constable said, roundly. "Whatever's left of the poor bugger is naked, probably because the killer knows it makes our jobs harder."

They had to agree; bodies that had been stripped of clothing and personal effects tended to have been the victim of an organised criminal gang who murdered as a matter of business, rather than sentiment.

"All right," Mel said, sucking some air through her teeth. "Let's take a look at what's left of him."

Jack instructed his body to remain calm, and not to fail him in front of two avid constables who expected a measure of decorum from a murder detective.

"Ready?" Melanie asked him.

"Mm hmm," he said, dubiously.

She crouched down beside the tarpaulin, drew on a pair of gloves and, taking a deep breath, lifted the edge.

Later, Jack would claim it was the heady smell of fish that tipped him over the edge, and not the visceral impact of seeing the sawn-off remains of what had once been a man, but, either way, his stomach emptied and there wasn't a single thing he could have done to stop it.

"I could murder a sausage sarnie."

With Ryan and Charlie engaged in the task of interviewing the conservation staff, Frank and Denise had been dispatched to talk to the staff who were resident on the Belsay estate. They'd set up a makeshift interview room in the kitchen, which was warm and carried the lingering scent of good food from the previous evening.

"Dream on," MacKenzie said, as they awaited the next interviewee. "You're on track to lose another pound this week, Frank, despite all those treats last night."

He nodded, gloomily. "I never said I couldn't have the body of a sculpted adonis if I wanted to," he said. "It's just that I've never *wanted* to."

She chuckled. "I see," she said, and turned to him with a glint in her eye. "Well, how about we get to the stage of you having the body of a sculpted sex object for my personal pleasure, and see if you find that a bit more appealing?"

Frank growled, and was about to pounce on her for a kiss, when there came a knock on the outer door.

"Come in!" she called out, with a sweet smile for her husband.

"I'll be back for you, later," he promised.

The door opened to admit an attractive woman in her early thirties, whose messy blonde hair had been caught up in a ponytail while the rest of her was wrapped up in warm, outdoor clothing in shades of bottle green, which indicated she was a member of the estate's gardening team.

"Come in, take a seat," Frank invited her, gesturing to a chair laid out at the big kitchen table opposite where he and Denise were already seated.

"Thanks," she said, fishing out a small packet of tissues so she could wipe her runny nose. "Sorry, it's so cold out there, today, my nose is adjusting to being in the warm."

They smiled, and went through the preliminaries, before settling down to ask a few questions.

"Can I have your full name, please?" Denise began, lifting her pencil to begin a new page of notes.

"Daisy Ann Flowers," she replied. "Before you say it, yes, my parents had a field day when they were naming me and my younger sisters. They're Rose and Lily, in case you're wondering."

They smiled again, liking the woman's easy manner.

"Might as well make the most of a surname like that," Denise agreed. "Would you mind telling us your occupation, here, and your address on the estate?"

Daisy nodded, and rattled off the name of one of the worker's cottages near the entrance to the driveway gates, which was around a mile's walk from the main hall.

"I'm an under-gardener here," she said. "It's a family tradition, really; my dad and grandad both worked the farms here on the estate, which is why my mum still has a tenancy at the cottage. Me and Henry—that's my son—we live with her, since my dad passed away last year, and I help out with the gardens when they need me."

"I'm sorry to hear it," Denise said, and Frank echoed the sentiment. "Is anyone else resident at the address?"

It was a polite way of asking about her marital situation, and she appreciated the attempt at being tactful.

"No, it's just me, mum and Henry," she replied. "Occasionally, my sisters come to stay with their families, but there isn't much room at the cottage, so we mostly go to stay with them. Henry's father died in Afghanistan; he was a Northumberland Fusilier."

They reiterated their condolences to a woman who'd lost two important men in her life, in quick succession.

"I have Henry," she said, with a smile. "Although he looks more like me than his dad." She lifted a shoulder, and tried to shake off the sadness. "Anyway, never mind all that, what about Kim? I couldn't believe it, when I heard what happened to her."

"Came as a bit of a shock to us, too," Frank murmured, and Denise gave him the side-eye, in her capacity as his senior in the police hierarchy.

"Did you know Kimberley well?" she asked.

Daisy shook her head. "No, not really," she replied. "Kim had only been on the estate for a few weeks, and she spent most of her time with the conservation team, as you'd expect. I said 'hello' to her a few times, and we were friendly, but that's the extent of it."

"How did she seem to you?"

"How d'you mean?"

"Her general mood and demeanour," Denise clarified.

"Oh…well, like I say, I really didn't know her very well," Daisy said, in a pained sort of voice. "She always seemed happy. In fact, she was someone I'd describe as vivacious, always laughing about something, or with a story to tell." She paused, thoughtfully. "Actually, come to think of it, she was a bit more subdued, when I saw her the other day."

"Yesterday?" Frank asked.

Daisy shook her head. "No, I didn't see her yesterday, it was the day before—on Saturday."

"What were the circumstances?"

"I was clearing some of the leaves from the front lawn, and I saw her heading towards the house, so I waved and said 'hello'," Daisy told them. "For once, she didn't wave back, although she saw me there."

"That was unusual?" Denise prodded.

"Yes, she was always very sociable, so I thought she must've been in a bad mood about something, but she didn't stop to talk or tell me anything that was on her mind, if that's what you're thinking."

They went through a number of other questions, circling back around to the same ones time and again to be sure they had everything Daisy could remember, before thanking her and wishing her a pleasant day.

Daisy hovered uncertainly, and they waited for her to say something else.

"What is it, pet?" Frank nudged her. "Have you remembered somethin' else?"

"No, it's just…I don't know if this is even something you're thinking of, but I have to tell you, she never struck me as someone who'd ever commit suicide. I know they say it could happen to anyone, and you can't always tell if someone's suffering, but…" She shrugged, and wrapped her arms around herself. "I just thought I'd tell you, Kim was the last person who'd ever take her own life, in my opinion."

Intuition, despite all its flaws and foibles, was often right, Denise thought. "Thank you," she said. "That's useful for us to know."

CHAPTER 11

Ryan was well aware that, in his line of work, to form value judgments before knowing anything about a person was a dangerous thing to do. There was every possibility his judgment could be wrong or at least not representative of the full picture. That being said, he'd never been wrong before, and, he'd go out on a limb and say that he wasn't wrong in that present moment, either.

Doctor Quentin Jones was a *gobshite*, as his dear sergeant would say.

He hadn't walked across the room, so much as swaggered; he hadn't smiled at them, so much as leered at Charlie, who was seated beside Ryan on one side of an old writing desk, in the room adjoining the library. *Ye Gods, he even looked like a fop*, with his thinning silver hair fashioned into a long, wavy style reminiscent of Richard Gere in the eighties, and—Ryan cringed inwardly—a gold signet ring on his pinkie finger.

Bloody hell.

Growing up, he'd known a lot of people who'd worn signet rings, many of them landed aristocracy, but, like his father before him, Ryan had instinctively known that he had no desire to look like a buffoon, and had therefore eschewed the practice.

"Is that your family crest?" he enquired of the man.

Jones crossed one chino-clad leg over the other, and they noticed he wasn't wearing socks with his tan leather loafers, despite there being ice on the ground outside.

"Hm? Oh, this old thing?" he said, flexing his fingers as though just noticing the ring was there. "It was a present from a grateful client, a few years ago."

He thought of a *memorable* few weeks he'd spent in the company of a rich widow in Hertfordshire, whose late husband no longer had any need of the little adornment, whereas he considered it payment for services rendered.

"Generous client," Charlie said.

"Yes, I've been fortunate to have worked with"—Jones paused, delicately—"*many* generous clients, over the years. They're always so grateful for the work that I and my team do, to bring their family history alive for them, you see. Often, they uncover secrets they knew nothing about, or find out about some medal or another their grandfather forgot to tell them about, before he died...you know the sort of thing."

Ryan cocked his head to one side. "Are you a petrol head, Doctor Jones?"

The other man flicked back his fringe and gave an elegant shrug. "I like cars, yes. Why do you ask?"

"I saw a particularly nice little racing number, sitting in the car park, earlier," Ryan said. "That wouldn't happen to be yours, would it?"

Jones bestowed another of his smug smiles. "Yes, the Merc's mine," he said. "Picked her up in Italy, after having her totally reconditioned."

"Must have cost an arm and a leg, if you don't mind me saying," Charlie remarked, playing the part of a wide-eyed young woman to perfection. "I wouldn't know about cars, myself."

Except how to change a tyre, check the engine, iron out dents, she added silently.

"It wasn't cheap," Jones admitted. "I'll let you sit in her, later, if you like. We could go for a spin—"

"*Very* kind of you," Ryan replied, as if the offer had been extended to both of them and not only to the pretty young woman by his side. "But we have a lot of work to get through; I'm sure you understand. Speaking of which, perhaps you can tell us about your colleague, Kimberley Foster?"

Jones re-crossed his legs, and began strumming his fingers against his knee. "What would you like to know?"

"Why don't you start from the top?" Ryan said, leaning back in his chair. "How and when did you first meet?"

Jones gave a negligent shrug of one linen-clad shoulder. "I advertised for a conservator-cum-archivist to join my team, back in the summer," he said. "The advert went out through several channels, including through the university careers services, which can often be helpful in finding young, *energetic* individuals."

Ryan eyed him with distaste, and thought again of making a value judgment about the man seated in front of them. "I see," he said, and he *did* see. "Kimberley was one of the applicants, I take it?"

"Yes, we discussed the job over the telephone and in person, and she joined the team a few weeks ago, in time to start the project here."

Ryan nodded. "I understand there are three permanent members of your team, plus two interns at any given time. Currently, that's you, Kim, Sabrina Fisher and two interns who come along for a full week from Northumbria University, but they change over weekly on a kind of rotation. Is that correct?"

Jones inclined his head. "Without wishing to be indelicate, we're down to two permanent members, now."

"Yes, I'm sure you were devastated to hear the news," he said, pointedly.

The doctor flicked his hair again, and Ryan told himself, rather sternly, that it would be a disproportionate response if he were to punch the man squarely in his preening face. He was sure the Chief Constable frowned upon that sort of thing, but the temptation was strong for him to suffer the consequences for the sheer pleasure of wiping the man's sneer off his insufferable face.

"Kim had some…*great* assets," Jones said, and his lip curled again. "She was a very good archivist, I must say. Diligent, hardworking…yes, she was full of surprises."

"Surely, that's why you hired her, in the first place?" Ryan pointed out.

"Oh—well, yes. Yes, of course."

Ryan and Charlie exchanged a telling glance, then returned to their questions.

"Did Kim have any cause to feel upset, lately?" Charlie asked him.

Jones stretched his arms behind his head, the very picture of a relaxed academic with the world at his feet. "Hardly," he scoffed. "She was paid over the odds to help to create a digital catalogue of all the Edgington family's artefacts, of which there are many. It may be time-consuming and repetitive, but it's not backbreaking. If anything, the work is quite interesting and varied; it can range from finding old fire extinguishers to plasterwork and doors, diaries and paintings, jewellery...the full spectrum."

They made a note, and he continued.

"As for her living conditions, the estate put us up in a row of little stone cottages for the duration of the project, which is well funded by the trust," he said. "All in all, detectives, I don't know what she could possibly have to feel upset about."

"What about her personal life?" Ryan asked, looking him dead in the eye. "What do you know about that?"

"She didn't have a boyfriend," he replied, and that much was true. "Look, she was just another twenty-something with a Masters in Conservation. We all got along very well, Sabrina included, and Kim never complained about anything to me. I'm sorry, I don't know what else to tell you."

But Ryan wasn't finished with him yet. "Do you know why Kim might have been up on the roof, last night?"

Jones shook his head. "No idea," he said. "She usually finished at five and, in any case, we don't work on the weekends."

"Did Kim have any enemies, Quentin?"

There was an infinitesimal pause before the doctor answered him.

"No," he said, firmly. "None that I know of."

The next person to walk into Ryan and Charlie's interview room was Doctor Jones' other young, female workmate. Sabrina Fisher was a slender redhead with big, blue eyes and, as the doctor would have said, other great assets besides the postgraduate degree she held in Conservation from a reputable, red-brick university.

"Thank you for coming in, Ms Fisher," Charlie said. "Please have a seat."

The woman looked distinctly nervous, they thought, with pale skin and deep shadows beneath her eyes which spoke of sleepless nights.

"Are you happy to answer a few questions for us, Sabrina?" He used her first name because it helped to build rapport with nervy subjects.

"Sure, no problem."

"Good," he said, and gave her a smile. "Can you tell us how you knew Kim Foster, please?"

Sabrina shifted uncomfortably. "Um, yeah, okay. Well, Kim joined the team not so long ago," she began. "This is a big job, so it was going to take another set of hands, and Quentin thought it was best to hire a third person. The interns come in, but they're mostly here to learn." She began playing with the ends of her hair. "So, yeah, Kim came along, and we all started here at the same time," Sabrina continued.

"Did you share a cottage?" Charlie asked.

"No, they gave us one each," she said, with a shrug. "I guess they've got plenty of space. They're the ones in a row, near the stables."

Ryan thought back to the general layout of the estate, which he'd studied in detail. "There's a farmhouse nearby as well, isn't there?"

Sabrina nodded. "Yeah, Paul lives there."

"Paul?"

"Yeah, Paul Bullman. He's the Head Gardener, or Groundskeeper, or whatever," she said.

"Okay, turning back to Kim," Ryan said. "If her cottage is next to yours, did you happen to notice when she left, last night?"

Sabrina shook her head. "No, I—I was watching telly—"

"Oh? What was on the box, last night? We missed it, being at the party," Charlie said, cheerfully.

Sabrina hesitated and fidgeted again. "Oh, just the usual Sunday night rubbish," she said, and gave a tinkling laugh. "But I'm sorry, I didn't hear Kim leave or anything like that."

"Do you have any idea why she might have been up on the roof, last night?" Ryan asked.

Sabrina relaxed again, clearly having found a more comfortable topic. "No," she said. "She might've been meeting someone, I suppose, but I don't know why anyone would meet up there."

"Perhaps she was working late?" Charlie suggested.

Sabrina rolled her eyes. "That'd be just like her, trying to show off to Quentin," she said, waspishly.

Ryan cocked his head to one side, interested to hear the sudden change in tone. "Did you and she have the same job remit?" he asked.

"It depends on what you classify as a 'job'," she returned, and then let out a sigh. "No, she was archiving things, whereas I'm writing the first draft of a history of Belsay, kind of like a ghostwriter for the new owner."

"Was it he who hired Quentin and the team?" Charlie asked.

"No, that was the estate trust," Sabrina said. "But I'm pretty sure Quentin's been in touch with the guy, to get a jump on things."

"What do you mean?"

Sabrina gave them both a look that told them clearly she thought they were naïve.

"You've met Quentin," she said. "He likes the finer things, and that costs money. He knows that he can upsell additional services, throw in a few extra charges and all that, and it'll be easier to do that if he speaks directly to some guy who probably can't even spell 'conservation', rather than trying to get one over on the trust's lawyers, down in London."

They nodded, and thanked her for the candour.

A few minutes later, she left, leaving Ryan and Charlie in a cloud of some expensive but cloying perfume.

"What d'you make of them?" he asked her.

Charlie thought for all of five seconds.

"I wouldn't trust either of them as far as I could throw them. What about you?"

"We're on the same page," he said. "They're hiding something…the question is, *what*?"

They fell silent, each thinking over what they'd heard so far, while dust motes circled the air in the old drawing room.

"We've a few interns to interview, then the catering and events staff to reinterview," Ryan said. "Frank and Denise are taking care of the other estate staff. Once we get through our list, what do you say to a quick recce of Kimberley's cottage?"

"I was going to suggest the same thing myself."

CHAPTER 12

Around lunchtime, Faulkner arrived at the Fish Quay and spotted Jack Lowerson looking distinctly the worse for wear.

"Uh-oh," he said. "Dodgy prawn, was it?"

"If by 'prawn' you mean 'body parts', and by 'dodgy' you mean 'bloated and ravaged by the sea', then yes," came the reply. "I'm never going to get that image out of my head."

"Distraction is key," Tom said. "You need to replace the image with something else."

"Like what?" Jack complained.

"Boobs," Tom said without thinking, and then, horrified at his professional slip, turned a shade of puce hitherto unknown in the medical profession.

"*What*?" Jack and Mel spoke in unison.

"I—um—I just mean—they're a good distraction," he burst out. "Nobody ever thinks of dead body parts when there's a pair of—well, you know—looking at you, or whatever—"

He fell silent, and the other two stared at him, agog.

"I don't think I've seen this side to you before, Tom," Melanie said, with a chuckle. "Then again, they do say it's the quiet ones. Do you have a particular *pair* you like to call to mind when trying to distract yourself from a gruesome scene?"

If possible, he turned an even more worrying shade of red.

"I'll take that as a 'yes'!" She giggled, all thoughts of rotting torsos momentarily forgotten.

"I agree," Jack said, smiling despite the fact his stomach continued to roll. "C'mon Tom, don't keep us in suspense. Are we talking about Pammy Anderson in her *Baywatch* era? Every teenage boy would agree with you—"

"No," Tom said, quietly. "In fact, I find I don't need to think about naked women to distract myself, any more."

"Commiserations," Jack said, earning himself a playful swipe from Melanie.

"So, what distracts you, nowadays?" she said.

Tom continued to step into his suit, focusing his attention on doing up the long zip that covered his everyday clothing beneath and would protect the forensic items from any further contamination, though he knew much of what might have been useful evidence would already have been lost to the sea.

"If you must know, I'm working up the courage to ask somebody on a date," he said, and prepared himself for an onslaught.

Instead, he was met with excitement.

It was well known that, after his divorce, Tom had struggled to find lasting love. For a while, he'd enjoyed a romance with a gardener up at Cragside, whom he'd met while working on a case up there, but when the job of a lifetime had been offered to her in another part of the world, he found himself unable to follow her. They'd had a great run, but life decisions tended to force your mind into sharp focus and, to his regret, they simply weren't destined to be 'forever'. Since then, he'd enjoyed a series of dates and short-lived relationships with some lovely, and some not-so-lovely, women, but he was coming to the realise something he'd always known, in the bottom of his heart.

He wanted long-term commitment.

He wanted somebody to cherish, to go home to, to work for, strive for, provide for, love and honour, protect and serve, as long as they both lived.

He hoped for a family, too, one day, and he wanted to enjoy playing with them before he was too old and decrepit to climb stairs, let alone play football.

"This is great!" Jack exclaimed, the prospect of matchmaking driving any residual nausea from his body. "Who's the lucky lady, eh? Oh, wait—wait—let me guess—"

"I'll bet it's Karen, from Digital Forensics," Mel offered. "I've seen her giving you the eye, Tom."

"Nah, she's got a fiancé." Jack tutted. "It's probably Daniella, that calls handler who tried to corner you at last year's party, after she got a load of you in the charity calendar—"

"She's seeing someone from Durham CID," Mel put in.

"Woah, there, cool your jets, Holmes and Watson," Tom laughed. "For your information, it's neither of them."

"Well, who, then?" Mel demanded, sticking her hands on her hips. "And, so help me, Tom, you'd better not tell us you fancy the Chief's new personal assistant, because she's terrifying."

He grinned, and shook his head. "I think you'll both approve," he said. "The question is whether my feelings would ever be reciprocated."

"Are you kidding? You're a great guy," Melanie said. "Don't do yourself down."

Jack smiled, and nodded his agreement. "So? Come on, feller. Dish the tea."

Tom gathered his courage, then remembered he was amongst friends who might laugh *with* him, but never *at* him. "Okay," he said, nervously. "Here goes nothing. It's... Charlie."

Jack stared at him, while his mind tried to compute the words. "Charlie...*our* Charlie? Charlie Reed?"

Melanie gave him a considering look, then turned to Faulkner with a big smile. "Oh, that's *great*, Tom," she said. "I don't know Charlie very well, but she seems really nice. You should definitely ask her out."

"Thanks," he said, breathing out a long sigh of relief. "I'm just working up the courage, as I say. In fact, I was wondering if I could ask a favour of you, Jack."

Lowerson came to attention, his mind having wandered along another pathway. "What's that?"

"I know you and Charlie are friends, and you know her pretty well," he said. "I was thinking…you know, maybe you could put in a good word for me? Tell her a few nice things, if you felt it was appropriate? I don't want you to tell her any lies, or embellish anything," he added quickly. "I'm not pretending to be anything other than what I am."

What he was, Jack realised, *was a thoroughly decent bloke.*

He was also awaiting a reply and, Jack realised, Melanie was, too.

"Of course I will," he managed, while a buzzing sound rang in his ears, and his heart plummeted to the pit of his stomach.

"Thanks, Jack, I really appreciate it."

"Don't mention it," he muttered, and wished the ground would swallow him alive.

By the time they'd finished interviewing the residents of Belsay, it was well after two o'clock and Charlie needed to leave, in order to make it back in time to collect Ben from his nursery school. There might have been a time when her mother had the strength to help look after her little boy for an hour or two in the afternoons, but that time had gone; she grew more fragile with every passing week, and Charlie didn't like to burden her with the added responsibility of taking care of a rumbunctious little boy with altogether too much energy to spare. Consequently, it was Phillips who joined Ryan at the front door of Kimberley's former cottage, having procured a key from Adrian, who could generally be found in the estate office.

"This is the one," Ryan said, and they followed a short, cobbled pathway to a painted front door covered in trailing ivy. It was the middle of three cottages, each of which was as pretty as a postcard, and comprised of two main rooms upstairs and downstairs, with a front and back door leading to a small yard area. From the front, they could see the stable block, and the far edge of the hall beyond it.

"Good view of things comin' and goin' from here," Frank said.

"Just what I was thinking," Ryan said, as he slid the door key into the lock. "Nobody we interviewed claimed to have any knowledge of why Kim was up on the roof, nor did they think she had any enemies or reason to be depressed or to want to take her own life."

"Same story with the people we talked to," Frank said. "None of the catering staff knew her, because they were drafted in from an external company. The on-site catering team is small, and they operate a tearoom for visitors to the hall out of the old kitchens, across the back courtyard. They'd seen her around, and she often popped in for lunch, but they kept to themselves."

Ryan pushed open the door to the cottage, and they stepped inside a narrow hallway painted in pale ivory, presumably to maximise the space. "What about the gardeners?" he asked. "Any luck, there?"

"We spoke to all of them except the head honcho," Frank replied. "Paul Bullman's the Head Gardener, but he didn't come for his interview, so he's the next one to track down."

"Apparently, he lives in the big farmhouse next door," Ryan said. "After we've finished looking around here, we'll pay Mr Bullman a visit."

"Very neighbourly," Frank agreed, and gave a husky laugh before turning his attention to their surroundings. "Nice little place, isn't it?"

Ryan nodded, and thought back to the cottage Anna had once owned, on the banks of the river in Durham. It had been small but perfectly formed, with keepsakes and artwork covering the walls, which were painted in warm, earthy shades of green that invited a person to relax and unwind. The cottage was no longer there, but the memories remained, and, as they moved through the small rooms with their thick stone walls, he was reminded of the happy times he and his wife had spent there together.

They moved through the rooms methodically, lifting cushions and other occasional items with gloved hands, careful not to touch anything that wasn't strictly necessary. They opened drawers and rifled through paperwork, until Ryan paused and turned to look at his friend.

"There was no handbag or anything like that, when I went up onto the roof," he said. "Do you remember if Pinter or Faulkner found any house keys in the pocket of

Kimberley's jeans, or in the jacket she was wearing when she fell?"

Phillips thought for a moment, then nodded. "She had a set of keys on her, on a keyring in the shape of the Rosetta Stone."

"If she'd been working late, there would have been more on her to find," Ryan said. "A bag, a leftover sandwich… something, wouldn't you think?"

"Aye, I would."

"In which case, it may be safe to assume she went up there without intending to stay very long."

"Unless it was a case of suicide, after all," Phillips pointed out. "She wouldn't have brought much with her, if she was thinking about ending it all."

Ryan nodded, then frowned at the empty living room, with its comfortable squishy sofa and local watercolours framed on the wall behind it. "I can't see a mobile phone anywhere."

"She probably left it upstairs," Frank said, but Ryan pulled a face that seemed to scream 'boomer' at him.

"Are you kidding?" he said. "Kim's from a different generation to you or me. They care about their phones the same way people care about their vital organs. There's no way she'd have left it lying around; she'd never be able to take pictures for Instagram, or scroll reels to find the perfect funny video to explain her mood. It's a way of life that may be alien to you and me, Frank, but it's a whole life concept to these kids."

Phillips thought of his daughter, and of the phone she kept asking for, day in, day out. "We're tryin' to hold off gettin' Sam her own phone," he said, in a voice intended to brook no argument, though, in this case, none was forthcoming. "The problem is, all her mates have got one, because the parents are weak buggers with more money than sense."

"Standard," Ryan muttered.

"Anyhow, it makes it hard to say to our lass that we care about her too much to see her mind reduced to mush, or to leave her open to online abuse, or any other kind of stress from havin' a bloody mobile phone strapped to her hip, all day, when these other parents are swannin' around buying phones for their kids. It's a bloody minefield, I'm tellin' you."

"Believe me, I'm dreading the teenage years," Ryan said, fervently. "The other night, I dreamed Emma turned up at the door with some kid called Alfie."

"I like the name Alfie."

"Frank, he was wearing braces, a gold hoop in his ear, and he was riding a unicycle."

"That changes things," Frank said, and barked out a laugh. "My advice would be to stay away from travelling dance or circus shows. That way, she'll meet a nice, steady bloke with a car, a decent pair of jeans and no piercings."

By this time, they'd completed their sweep of the downstairs, which took no time at all, and had ascended the staircase to the first floor, where the master bedroom was the first door at the top of the landing. They rooted around Kim's wardrobe, had a look under the bed and beneath piles of dirty laundry, until they came to the bedside table on what they assumed was her regular side of the bed. Frank tugged open a drawer, and made a comedy sound in the back of his throat.

"Are you having a stroke?" Ryan asked him.

"Not yet," Phillips replied. "But it may not be far off. Come and see this."

Ryan walked around the bed and peered down into the bedside drawer, which was laden with junk, but one thing jumped out at them from its resting place atop a pile of condoms and lubricant.

A pair of handcuffs.

"Well, I never would have guessed," Frank declared, reaching for the cuffs. "Who'd have known she was an undercover agent? I wonder if her warrant card's around here, somewhere."

"Frank," Ryan said, and tried hard not to laugh. "There are other reasons why people sometimes keep handcuffs in their bedside drawer. Besides which, when have you ever seen a set of police-issued restraints with pink fluff on them?"

Phillips looked again at the handcuffs, then at his friend, and finally, off into the middle distance. "I wonder if—"

"Don't say it, Frank."

"I was only going to ask—"

"So help me, I'll strangle you with your own tie, if you ask me where you can buy a pair of these."

Phillips folded his lips, and wondered if there might be a receipt knocking around somewhere. "Well, we can assume one thing," he said.

Ryan eyed him with nervous suspicion. "What?"

"Kim was either *gettin'* her leg o'er, or she was *expectin'* to get it o'er, judgin' by the sheer number of condoms she's got in here. I mean, hell's teeth, did she get them on a bulk deal or what?"

"As ever, a charming turn of phrase," Ryan said. "We're not here to judge the victim's sexual appetite, sergeant."

"Where's the fun in that?" Phillips countered. "In any case, that's exactly what we're here for. How are we gonna find out who did for her, if we don't know who she was bumpin' uglies with?"

It was a fair point.

"Promise me something, will you, Frank?"

Phillips waited.

"Never, *ever* use the phrase, 'bumping uglies' within my earshot, again, or I'll have you packed off to the back end of beyond faster than you can say, 'traffic duty'. All right?"

Phillips laughed, and wondered if it was a good time to mention the second set of handcuffs he'd just discovered in the other bedside table.

Probably not, he decided.

CHAPTER 13

Around the time Ryan was feeling decidedly queasy at the thought of his two good friends bumping uglies, Anna was feeling equally unsettled. She knelt beside the toilet bowl, having been sick several times throughout the morning. Her mother-in-law hovered in the corridor outside, and called to her through the keyhole.

"Can I come in, dear?"

"Yes—come in!"

Eve opened the bathroom door, where she found Anna propped up against the porcelain looking tired and washed out, her face pale and sickly after several rounds of vomiting. "Oh, you poor thing," she said, and hurried to retrieve a glass of water and a cool washcloth. "Is it the painkillers, do you think? They can be very strong, sometimes…"

"I—I don't know what it is," Anna said, and felt another round of sickness rise up in her belly. "Oh, no—"

A few minutes later, Eve helped her back into bed. "I'm going to get you a nice cup of tea," she said.

"And, I know you won't feel like eating, but I'm going to make you some toast, anyway, just in case you can manage a couple of bites. You need to keep your strength up, in your condition."

Condition?

Anna's head had just touched the pillow, but it flew back up again, jarring her sore shoulder.

"My condition," she repeated, while her mind whirred. "I—I'm not—at least, I don't think so—"

She fell quiet, performing a quick calculation of dates in her head. To her astonishment, it had been more than six weeks since her last period, but life had been so busy she simply hadn't noticed.

"I might be," she whispered, and her eyes shone. "I wasn't this sick the last time, with Emma—"

"Every child is different," Eve said gently, coming to perch on the bed and wrap her arms around Anna's trembling shoulders. "Max—Ryan, I should say—and Natalie were both *entirely* different. He gave me a lot of sleepless nights kicking me every which way, whereas his sister seemed a lot more peaceful throughout. That's boys and girls for you, I suppose."

"I think I have a pregnancy test left over in the bathroom cupboard," Anna said, throwing back the covers. "I'll get it, and see what happens."

Eve put a hand over hers. "I'll be here, either way."

Anna smiled, and reached out to give her mother-in-law another hug. Having lost her own mother many years ago, she'd never dreamed she'd be fortunate enough to find a woman with enough kindness and generosity of spirit to love her and treat her like a daughter—especially since Eve had lost her own. Yet, here they were, two souls who'd found one another and forged a strong, loving bond.

"Thank you, Eve," she whispered, and squeezed her a little tighter. "I'll be back in a moment."

Ryan's mother waited until the bathroom door closed before doing a little jig on the spot, then she told herself not to count any chickens, just yet. There was every chance Anna was simply unwell, and they shouldn't read too much into morning sickness.

Still…

She thought of another grandchild, and could already imagine its downy hair and soft, baby skin…It was only a few minutes, yet it seemed an eternity until the door opened again and Anna leaned against the frame, pregnancy test still clutched in one hand.

"Well?" Eve whispered. "Should I start knitting?"

A slow smile spread over Anna's face, and then she nodded.

Oblivious to the fact his life was about to change all over again in approximately nine months' time, Ryan locked the door to Kimberley's cottage and tucked the key inside his jacket pocket.

"Couldn't see any sign of a mobile phone anywhere in the house," Phillips said. "We looked everywhere, n'all."

Ryan nodded, and then smiled at his friend.

"What're you grinnin' about?"

"I'm smiling, because our instincts were proven right again," he replied. "Why would Kim's mobile phone be missing unless a third party disposed of it?"

"She might not have one, or she might've left it somewhere," Phillips argued, but it sounded weak, even to his own ears.

"Whoever took it made a serious mistake, because now we *know* she didn't fall accidentally," Ryan said. "If they'd left well alone, we might've concluded that she'd suffered an accident, and whoever pushed her could've got away with it. Now, because they've taken that phone, we know there's something and someone to find."

Phillips nodded, and they began walking from the cottages towards the stone farmhouse, a short distance away. Like the workers cottages, it overlooked the stable complex but, from its position, could also see the front of the hall, though he imagined the view would be obstructed in the summer when the trees were in bloom.

"I love these old walls," Frank confessed, and ran his palm over stone that had been quarried right there on the estate, used to build the new hall and its cottages. An impressive quarry garden had been fashioned from its skeleton, with its own micro-climate to support the exotic plants that were meticulously tended by an extensive team led by the man they'd come to find.

They knocked on the front door of the farmhouse, and waited for an answer.

"What's the name of the Head Gardener, again?" Phillips asked.

"Paul Bullman," Ryan replied. "He's been at Belsay for nearly thirty years."

"I wonder how he'll take to having a new owner on site, after havin' a free hand for so long," Phillips said.

"I'd have liked to ask him, but it seems nobody's home." Ryan cupped his hands together and peered through one of the downstairs windows, but the rooms were in darkness.

"Well, let's take the key to Kimberley's cottage back to the estate office, and decide where to go from there," Phillips suggested.

Ryan agreed, and the pair made their way across the open courtyard, past the stables towards the kitchen entrance. However, rather than stopping for a fruit scone with clotted cream, as Frank might have liked, they veered in the other direction towards the servants' wing of the hall and the old estate office. As they approached, they heard Adrian's low, rumbling voice, as well as another male voice they didn't recognise.

Ryan rapped a knuckle against the open door and stepped inside, with Phillips in tow.

"Ah, Chief Inspector, sergeant," Adrian said, rising from the old captain's desk to usher them both inside the large, faded room with its old metal filing cabinets and enormous framed map of Belsay and its surrounds. "This is Paul Bullman, our Head Gardener."

They turned to look at Bullman, a short, stocky man in bottle green canvas trousers and a matching fleece.

"Just the man we were looking for," Ryan said. "I must congratulate you—the gardens are spectacular."

"My old da was groundskeeper here, before he died," Bullman said, with a shrug of his burly shoulders. "He's the one who had a real talent for landscapin'. I'm just carryin' on his work, you might say."

Ryan wasn't sure whether the reply was humble, dismissive, or both. "We were hoping to ask a few questions of you, when you have a moment?" he said.

"No bother," Bullman said, and bobbed his chin in the direction of the farmhouse visible through the window. "If you want to find me, I only live across the way, in the farmhouse over there."

Ryan didn't bother to mention they'd already tried to find him, for, at that moment, there came another knock at the door.

"It's like a revolvin' door, today," Adrian said, half to himself. "Come in!"

Presently, there appeared in the doorway a man none of them had ever met.

"Mark Newman," he said, and held out a hand to each of them. "I'm the owner, so they tell me."

He had a soft Australian accent but, even without it, they might have guessed his provenance. Tall, well-built and with a crop of honey-blond hair, he looked as though he'd found himself lost on the way to the nearest beach.

"Welcome to Belsay," Adrian said. "I've been the acting estate manager here for a number of years—we spoke on the phone, the other day."

Newman nodded, and his eyes flicked to the other three men in the room.

"This is DCI Ryan and DS Phillips, from Northumbria Police, and this is our Head Gardener, Paul Bullman."

"Right," Newman said, nodding to each of them before turning back to Ryan and Phillips. "Sorry, did you say you'd come from the *police*?"

They nodded, and Ryan proceeded to explain the reason they were there. "I'm sorry your first visit to Belsay is tainted by death," he concluded.

"Yes, I've just come up from London, by way of Yorkshire," Newman muttered. "A little bolthole in Richmond came as part of the estate, so I thought I might as well stop in here on my way north—"

"Richmond's a lovely place," Phillips threw in. "They've got a *crackin'* pie shop—"

Ryan gave him a long look, and he clamped his gob shut.

"I'm sorry to hear about the young woman who died," Newman said. "Was her death some kind of work-related accident? Do I need to…*do* anything? I have to be honest… I'm new to all of this. Until the lawyers got in touch a few months ago, I had no idea I was in line to inherit *any* of this." He spread his hands wide, to encompass their surroundings, then ran agitated hands through his mop of hair. "I mean, look at this place!" he exclaimed. "I had a meeting with the administrators, while I was in London, but I was still jet-lagged and a lot of it went over my head. The heretofores and all that legal lingo might as well be Portuguese, for all I understand of it."

Ryan smiled, but it didn't quite reach his eyes. "I'm sure you'll feel at home here, sooner than you think," he said. "To answer your first question, I'm afraid we have some doubts about whether Kimberley's fall was accidental. It's far more likely she was pushed."

The three men stared at the two police officers with expressions of comical surprise.

"But—*why*?" Newman said, aghast. "Why would anyone want to push her?"

"That's what we'll be working hard to find out," Ryan replied. "Can we rely on your full support during the course of our investigation?"

Newman bobbed his head, still looking shell-shocked. "Of course," he said. "Anything to help…this is *awful* news. Have—have her parents been contacted? Should I—?"

"That's been taken care of, Mr Newman," Frank assured him.

He nodded, obviously relieved to hear it. "All the same, I'd want to send some flowers…whatever you think best."

"I'm sure they'd appreciate that."

Newman ran a tongue over his teeth, and tried to put his next thought as delicately as he could. "The team have been trialling a new programme of events, here at Belsay," he said. "For the first time, the Trust has opened up the main house for private dinners, wedding breakfasts and that sort of thing. I'm inclined to continue the idea when I take up residence and, with that in mind, it would be best to avoid any negative publicity. I don't suppose...is there any way of keeping this out of the press? The last thing I need is a murder putting people off."

Ryan's face remained impassive, but his voice was firm.

"I'm sorry, Mr Newman. We'll do our best to be as discreet as possible, but we can't always prevent information leaking to outside sources. I'm sure you understand that our main priority is coming to understand the circumstances of Ms Foster's death, for her family's sake."

Newman nodded, miserably.

"Adrian," Ryan said, turning back to the man who knew most about the day-to-day operations of the estate. "I understand there's only one main driveway in and out of the estate—is that correct?"

"There's a couple of other estate access lanes," he told them, and swung around to point at a large plan of the grounds mounted on the wall behind his desk. The paper was old beneath the glass frame, and the date at the bottom told them it had been completed in January of 1908.

He indicated the exits, and Ryan thought of the video footage his team had taken of the immediate vicinity surrounding the hall, the previous evening. There had been no significant tyre tracks through the snow, other than along the main driveway. However, that didn't rule out the possibility of someone driving along a back road, parking their vehicle a safe distance out of sight of the main complex, and then covering the rest of the distance on foot—

"If you're wondering whether an outsider snuck in and snuck out again, they would've had to use the main driveway," Bullman said, and they all turned to face him.

"Why d'you say that?" Frank asked.

"Weren't any tracks on the back roads, last night, were there?" Bullman said, as if it were obvious. "If someone came in from outside, they would've had to use the main driveway." He scratched the side of his chin, then folded his arms. "Unless they hiked o'er the snow," he added, as an afterthought. "Could've left their car in one of the lay-bys on the main road that runs along the edge of the estate, then hopped a fence and made their way across the fields, cross-country, like."

Ryan looked at the map, estimating the distance involved. "The snow was several inches deep, last night," he said, turning back to the others. "It would've been quite an effort to hike over the fields, wouldn't it?"

"Would've been a canny hike," Bullman admitted. "Like I say, it would've been a lot easier for someone to have come up the main driveway. You'd have to be mad, otherwise."

"Sounds about right," Frank said, and then muttered something dark about fruitcakes with a penchant for the Great Outdoors.

"I think Paul's right," Adrian said, after a moment. "It just doesn't make sense for anyone wanting to make a quick getaway to try and plough through the snow when it would've been easier—and faster—to use the existing tracks along the main driveway."

"Do CCTV cameras cover all access points?" Ryan asked him.

Adrian's gaze moved briefly towards the estate's new owner, and then back to the Chief Inspector. "No," he said, mildly. "I would've liked to have new cameras installed, but the Trust deemed it unnecessary since we already have a number of old cameras that can be repaired or reconditioned. Unfortunately, we haven't yet had an opportunity to do that, and the ones that do work were severely obscured by the snowfall."

"All the same, we'd like to see the footage from last night."

Adrian nodded. "I'll see to it."

"What if…" Newman spoke hesitantly, having considered another more troubling possibility. "I was only thinking…if you're right, and Kimberley *was* pushed to her death…what if it wasn't an outsider who came into the hall and then scarpered again? What if it was…" He broke off, looking uncomfortable.

"What if it was someone already inside?" Ryan finished for him, softly.

The other man nodded.

"Yes," Ryan said. "I've been wondering the same thing."

CHAPTER 14

While Ryan and Frank dug further into the life of the late Kimberley Foster, Jack and Melanie oversaw the transfer of human remains from the dockside at North Shields to the mortuary at the Royal Victoria Infirmary. A wide cordon had been erected to prevent any rubberneckers muscling their way through the gathering crowd while the remains were bagged and transported by a pair of sombre-looking technicians and, disappointed not to have caught a glimpse, the looky-loos eventually dispersed.

Melanie watched the last of them wander off in search of fried fish, and wondered whether she could stomach a bite to eat, since it was past lunchtime. "Shall we head over to the fish shop and have a word with the owner?" she asked of Jack, who walked beside her, lost in thought. "I could probably manage a few chips, now it's over and done with."

Jack made a non-committal sound in the back of his throat. "If you like."

Mel glanced at him, then down at the wooden decking beneath her sensible walking boots. "What d' you reckon about the body parts?" she asked. "Professional or amateur job?"

Jack thought about it. "Could be either," he said. "I'd lean more towards a professional killing but, if they aren't buried or drowned in acid, remains are usually weighted down more thoroughly than those were. The idea is for them not to be found too quickly."

Mel grimaced, but nodded her agreement. "The cuts were clean," she said. "Whoever dissected the body knew exactly where to make the incisions, and had the right sort of tools to perform the task neatly. That suggests to me a perp who's either inexperienced but confident and well prepared, or someone who's had plenty of experience in that line of work."

"Neither option is particularly appealing," Jack had to say.

Mel nodded. "I know what you mean," she said. "It takes a certain kind of personality to handle a body like that. Somebody like—"

"Jeff Pinter?"

She cast a surprised glance in his direction, then nodded slowly. "Yeah," she said. "Somebody like Jeff, if he was a killer rather than a forensic pathologist."

"Both occupations need the same detachment, don't you reckon?" Jack said, thoughtfully. "They say there's a higher percentage of psychopathic personality types in medical professions and, let's face it, we've known a few dodgy doctors in our time."

She smiled. “You’re not wrong, but, don’t forget, there’s an equal number in the police force, so they say. Deviant personality types without empathy or remorse are often attracted to positions where they can exert significant power. It makes sense, when you think about it.”

“It would keep me up at night, if I thought about it too much,” he shot back. “Next, you’ll be telling me Frank keeps a stash of bodies in his basement.”

“There’d be no room, what with all the boxes of Turkish Delight he probably has stashed down there already.”

Jack smiled, finding it all too easy to imagine.

“Joking aside,” Mel continued, “Frank’s in the best shape I’ve seen him in years. How did he manage it? I always thought wild horses couldn’t drag him away from the Pie Van.”

“It’s about finding the right motivation,” Jack replied. “He has Samantha and Denise to think of, especially after his heart scare.”

Mel stopped dead outside the fish shop. “Heart scare? What heart scare?”

Jack searched her face and realised she had no idea what had happened. “I—Mel, I told you all about it, in my e-mails,” he said, unable to keep the hurt from his voice. “There was a car bomb outside Frankland Prison that was meant for Ryan, but Frank was caught in the blast instead and it brought on a cardiac arrest. He managed to pull through, but it gave all of us a good scare.”

Mel frowned, and looked away. "I'm sorry, Jack. I must have missed that message," she said. "I sort of went… off grid, I suppose. I sometimes left it a few weeks before checking messages or replying—"

"If you replied, at all," he said, before he could stop the words from tumbling out of his mouth. Then, he shook his head. "It doesn't matter." He reached for the door to the fish shop, but she put a hand on his arm to stop him.

"It matters," she argued. "I mean it when I tell you I'm sorry, Jack. I bitterly regret ever having to leave you, our home, and the life we built together. I wish I'd been in a better place, one where I was able to just—to just *cope* with what happened." Mel drew in a shaky breath, and carried on. "But I couldn't get past the nightmares," she said. "I couldn't switch off the memories, the flashbacks… everything reminded me of *him*." A small shudder passed through her body. "I needed to know I could survive on my own, even if there was nobody there to help me," she said. "Even while I was away, I could feel myself starting to rely on getting your e-mails, like a lifeline, but that defeated the object. I wanted to hear from you, Jack, even while I knew I needed to go cold turkey. I don't know if you can understand that."

"I can," he said, and heaved a sigh that was a mixture of frustration and regret. "I didn't know if I was doing the right thing, e-mailing you every week. I suppose, I hoped it would help to preserve a bond between us, despite the distance. It was…" He swallowed a sudden, painful lump in his throat. "It was cathartic for me," he managed to say. "I needed to write to you, Mel. I was going mad, wondering how you were doing, and if you were safe."

"I was so wrapped up in my own feelings, I didn't stop to think about how it was affecting other people," she said, with dawning realisation. "It was selfish of me, and I'm sorry."

"You don't have anything to be sorry for," he said. "I'm the one who needs to be sorry. You asked for space, but I didn't give it to you, and then blamed you when you didn't respond in the way I wanted you to. I should have thought of your needs above my own…"

Mel stepped forward, and took his hands in hers. "How about a fresh start?" she said.

Jack searched the lines of her face, and knew that they'd come to a crossroads. He opened his mouth to say something, he wasn't sure what, when Fate interceded once again.

"DC Lowerson? DC Yates?"

Mel dropped his hands, and they turned to find one of the local constables jogging towards them, looking distinctly green around the gills.

"Everything alright, Potter?"

"It's the forensic team, sir. They've found another bit of body, washed up beneath the dock."

He swallowed, hard.

Jack and Mel exchanged a rueful glance, while the prospect of lunch evaporated.

CHAPTER 15

While the semi-decomposed remains of a male femur were fished out of the water, Ryan and Phillips made their way from Belsay Hall towards the city centre, having heard that their police pathologist had looked over the body of Kim Foster and was ready to impart his forensic wisdom. As they motored across town with Ryan's hands at the wheel, Frank distracted himself from thoughts of impending calamity with a little help from Magic FM.

"This one's a banger!" he declared, as Kim Wilde began to sing about kids in America.

Ryan glanced across at his friend and smiled. "I thought you were more of a seventies man?" he said. "The Jackson Five, Abba…that sort of thing."

All thoughts of road traffic accidents momentarily banished, Phillips took refuge on the safe ground of classic music from his hey-day.

"You're not wrong," he said, folding his fingers across his shrinking belly. "I'll never turn down a dance to *Super Trouper*, and don't get me *started* on Boney M—"

"No fear of that," Ryan muttered, and accelerated across a mini-roundabout while there was a momentary gap in traffic.

"That being *said*," Frank continued, once his stomach had settled back in its usual place, "There's nowt like an eighties power ballad to get your blood pumpin'. As for Kim Wilde…I had a proper crush on her, back in the day. Her, and Sinitta," he added. "And Kate Bush—" He patted a hand against his chest.

Ryan grinned, and tried to imagine his sergeant ever being young enough to experience a crush. "Anna loves eighties music, too," he said, blithely undertaking a slow-moving ambulance with its blue lights flashing. "She's more of a Springsteen fan…so am I, for that matter. She loves Def Leppard, Bon Jovi, Guns 'n' Roses…"

"All respectable choices," Phillips pronounced, and began to hum *Streets of Philadelphia*. "Speakin' of your better half, how's she doin' after last night?"

"She was in a bit of pain, this morning," Ryan replied. "My mum's still with us, at the moment, so at least I know someone's there in case she needs help with anything, especially when it comes to handling Emma."

Frank smiled at the thought of his friend's daughter. "Aye, she's a firecracker, that un," he chuckled. "Wouldn't fancy bein' in your shoes when she hits sixteen!"

"Yours is going to be there, soon enough," Ryan tossed back at him.

"Bugger," Frank said, and both men laughed before Phillips became serious again. "How's your ma, after everythin' that happened?"

Ryan indicated and performed a left turn before replying, giving himself a moment to consider his response. "She misses my father, terribly," he said, and then added, "We all do."

Phillips put a hand on his shoulder in silent support.

"It's been a good thing for her, coming to stay with us for a while," Ryan continued. "We've tried to persuade her to stay longer, or even to come and live with us, if she wants to, but…" He swore softly, as a white van almost took them out. "She's too attached to Summersley," he continued. "It's home, and has been home for a very long time. Besides, she isn't ready to leave my sister or my father."

They were both buried in the quiet splendour of his family's mausoleum, Frank knew. "Aye, I can understand that," he said, thinking of his first wife's grave and whether it was time to pay her a visit. "How'll she manage the estate, though? It's a big old rambling place for just one person."

"I've spoken to her, and I think she'd like to open the place up for good causes," Ryan said. "Events to support a charity, for instance, or artists' retreats for wellbeing or grief recovery. My mother was a talented watercolour painter, and still is. She used to teach art therapy at a local outreach centre for years."

The hospital came into view, and he began to slow the car.

"In terms of the estate, I'm recruiting for a new estate manager, since the old one retired," Ryan continued. "Once that's done and we have someone who knows how to take care of that kind of complex, I won't need to worry so much about the day-to-day running. She has housekeeping help, and gardeners, but the nights will be lonely. If she's determined to stay on there, then it could be a good idea to invite my aunt to visit for a while, or one of my cousins."

Frank turned to him in surprise. "I didn't know you had other family!" he said, but then realised he must have met them, at Natalie Ryan's funeral years before. It had been a sad and difficult day for everyone, and his focus had been on supporting his friend rather than scrutinising the other guests. Ryan and Anna's wedding had been an intimate affair but, now he thought of it, he remembered a few attractive, well-dressed, 'upper-crusty' types who'd mellowed into being half-decent craic once they'd necked a few glasses of bubbly.

"Yes, I have an aunt, Helen, on my father's side and another one on my mother's side, Olivia," Ryan explained. "They each have two children apiece, all roughly my age."

"Do you see them often?"

Ryan lifted a shoulder. "Family weddings, birthdays, that sort of thing," he replied. "My Aunt Helen was always closest to us, growing up. She's a few years younger than my father, so they didn't have all that much in common, or so I've always thought. She was more of a tearaway, at school, whereas my father followed rules to the letter—"

Ryan thought of a few of the entries he'd read from his father's old diaries, and found himself wondering whether Charles Ryan had been so much of a stickler for convention, after all. There was so much still to learn about his father, he realised, and it was a tragedy that he was only really doing it once the man had passed away.

"Anyway," he said, swinging the car into a space Frank could have sworn was too small, but turned out to be a perfect fit, before bringing the engine to a stop. "I think we'll have to see how things go, over the next few months. We'll visit her as often as we can, and she's promised to come up every few weeks to see us—although it's mostly to see Emma, I'm sure." Ryan smiled, thinking of how his child adored her grandmother. "How are you settling into the new digs?" he asked his friend, before they squeezed themselves out of the car doors.

"To the manor born," Frank declared. "O' course, we hardly see our offspring. Samantha's in her element, being so close to the stables. It's a wonder she doesn't just move in with that bloomin' horse."

Ryan smiled. "And Denise? Is she enjoying country life?"

"Ask a daft question," Frank said. "She's swannin' round the place like Lady Muck, tellin' muggins here to mind my feet on the sofa and all sorts. Next, she'll be brandishin' a ridin' crop—"

Ryan snorted. "You wish," he said, smartly. "Come on, Muggins. We've got work to do."

CHAPTER 16

There was a chill in the air as they crossed the forecourt of the Royal Victoria Infirmary and made their way through its automatic doors. As always, the lobby bustled with activity and, much like police headquarters, was an eclectic mix of British society, covering every age from newborn to elderly; every race and ethnicity; every sex and, they imagined, many more distinguishing features besides. They congregated seeking care, reassurance and, in some cases, simply for the company of other human beings, because loneliness may not have been a physical complaint, but it could certainly be the catalyst.

The two detectives raised a hand in greeting to one or two of the staff they recognised, having walked along the rubber-coated corridors of the hospital more times than either of them could count. It was a source of joy and sorrow, being at once the place where Ryan's child had been born, and where he'd once apprehended a serial killer known as 'The Hacker', before giving chase to Keir Edwards along the very same corridor they now followed. Likewise, they'd attended any number of suspicious cases, fatalities and grievous injuries, discounting the ones they'd sustained in the line of duty.

"If only these walls could talk, eh?" Phillips murmured.

"They'd tell us to think about another line of work," Ryan said, and his friend laughed.

They took the stairs down to the basement and headed in the direction of the mortuary, a route they would have known even with their eyes closed. As they drew nearer, the temperature in the corridor became noticeably warmer, which was the result of a series of high-level, aluminium air ducts attached to the air conditioning system that kept the mortuary space cool. In exchange, it pumped stuffy air into the corridor outside.

"Gordon Bennett!" Frank complained. "It's hotter than Satan's arse crack, down here!"

"Charming, as ever," Ryan drawled.

"Aye, well, you were thinkin' it," Phillips grumbled. "Aw, howay man, don't tell us he's changed the bloody key code again?"

They'd come to a standstill outside a set of double security doors, which blocked access to the mortuary space to those not in possession of a magic, four-digit numerical key code.

"It's always a memorable date, to do with some public figure who's died in the past," Ryan said, and ran an irritable hand through his dark hair while he tried to recall whom it could possibly be. "Pinter told me who it was, at the dinner the other night. Give me a minute—"

Phillips stood, lips pursed, and waited for divine inspiration to strike. "Let's look at this, logically," he said, when a few minutes had passed without any lightning bolt. "The last time, it was Freddie Mercury, which you remembered because he'd been listening to a lot of Queen's Greatest Hits. What's he been playing, lately? Maybe it'll give us a clue."

"Good thinking—"

Ryan snapped his fingers. "He was listening to Amy Winehouse's *Back in Black* last week, and I'm sure he was playing *Valerie* when we popped in the other day," he said. "It must be her. Now, when did she die?"

Phillips tried to remember. "Mid-noughties?" he hazarded a guess.

"It must have been while I was still living in London," Ryan muttered, thinking back to what felt like another lifetime. "I'm going to try 2011."

He keyed in the numbers and, a second later, the doors buzzed open.

"You've been readin' those Trivial Pursuit cards again, haven't you?"

"I do little else," Ryan said, and held open the door.

Stepping inside Pinter's domain, they found they were not the only police personnel in attendance that day.

Durham Police Constabulary had seen a bit of staff turnover during the previous couple of years, following allegations of corruption within the ranks and a general clear-out of 'bad blood', but, despite an influx of new faces they recognised the man and woman dressed in visitors' lab coats as being their counterparts from the Major Crimes team in the neighbouring county.

"DCI Nicholls and DS Baker," Ryan said. "What brings you to our neck of the woods?"

He reached for a clipboard beside the door and signed his name on the visitor log before passing it to Frank.

"Ryan, Phillips, it's good to see you both." The more senior of the two, Jan Nicholls, stepped forward and held out her hand. "We need a second opinion on a body we found the other week, so Pinter's agreed to look it over for us. How's tricks?"

"Steady," Ryan replied, and shook Baker's hand as he came over to join them. "Chris, good to see you—it's been a while."

"Aye, it has," he said, and pumped Ryan's hand, then Frank's. "What brings you both down to the fridges?"

"Female, late twenties," Ryan said, vaguely. "You?"

"Female, mid-fifties," Baker replied, equally sparing of detail. "Looked accidental, at first glance, but..." She trailed off, and left the rest unsaid.

"Something doesn't fit?" Ryan finished for her, with a smile. "We know that feeling, don't we, Frank?"

"Aye, whenever I try and fit into me old jeans," came the pithy reply.

"You're lookin' well, lad," Baker told him. "You been boxin' again?"

"Aye, I can still go a few rounds," Frank replied, modestly. "You keepin' up with it, yourself?"

"When I can," the other man replied, and patted his paunch. "Gotta shift this spare tyre after Christmas."

"If you fancy sparrin' a bit, give us a shout," Frank said, and they chewed the fat for another minute or two, before Nicholls nudged her partner.

"Sorry to break things up, but we best be on our way," she said. "Nice runnin' into you both, and, if I don't see you again, have a happy Christmas and New Year."

She raised a hand towards Pinter, who had taken a call from another department and waved a distracted hand in return. While he completed his phone call, Ryan and Phillips hovered beside the doorway, as far from the immersion tanks and cold storage drawers as they could manage without looking like a pair of cowardy custards.

"Don't often need a second opinion, these days," Frank mused. "Wonder why they've come out of jurisdiction, n'all."

Ryan smiled to himself. "And you accuse me of imagining dark deeds around every corner," he said. "It could be as simple as the defence team requesting a second postmortem, which they're entitled to do. On the other hand, the first one might have been contaminated in some way or another...as for Pinter, as much as it pains me to admit it, you and I both know he's the best and, technically, he's a freelancer. He can work for whichever constabulary he likes."

Phillips made a raspberry sound, to convey his thoughts as far as other constabularies went. Broadly, they matched his thoughts regarding football teams: he was sure the others had a lot to recommend themselves, but nothing compared with the Magpies.

"*Gents*," Pinter said, sounding a bit like an extra from a Guy Ritchie movie as he swaggered towards them. "Sorry to keep you waiting, there's been a rush on the mortuary today."

It was an uncomfortable turn of phrase, and Frank wrinkled his nose.

"I've had a look at the young lady who fell through the ceiling, last night," he continued. "I've put her in one of the private examination rooms, through here."

He led them from the main area and along a narrow corridor leading to several private offices, a small laboratory facility and four private examination rooms. He keyed in the access code for one of them and led them both inside a spotlessly clean room illuminated by jarringly bright overhead strip lighting. A workstation was set against one wall, more cold storage drawers covered the back wall, and, in the centre of it all, a shrouded body lay inert on a metal gurney.

"Here she is," Pinter said, as if he was introducing them to a new acquaintance. "Apologies for the smell in here, one of the extractors is out of order and I'm still waiting for the maintenance team to come and fix it."

They nodded, and tried not to inhale too much of the sickly, lemon-infused air that carried the over-ripe flavour of fruit gone bad mingled with bodily gases and preservative chemicals.

Ryan cleared his throat. "So, what can you tell us?"

The pathologist peeled back the shroud to reveal what had once been Kimberley Foster. "Let's see," he said, gathering his thoughts. "Twenty-five years old and in generally good health, when she died. I'm waiting for her toxicology report to come back from the lab, but there's nothing to suggest drug use—or *abuse*—and no other signs of long-term addiction."

He indicated the skin on her arms, legs and even her feet, which was smooth and unblemished by track marks or any other scarring aside from a small tattoo of the moon and stars on her abdomen.

"Obviously, her nails and hair follicles might tell a different story, but I'll update you," he said. "As for blood alcohol levels, she was clean."

"Which would rule out any idea of her being intoxicated and falling while drunk or high," Ryan said.

Pinter nodded.

"As for other basic information, she'd ingested a ham and cheese sandwich on white bread, with some butter, roughly an hour before she died," he continued. "Nothing untoward in her stomach, but I'll update you if we find anything toxic in the samples. As for her organs, she had good muscle tone, good teeth, and her vascular system reflected a generally healthy diet, which we'd hope to see for someone her age. Aside from the trauma brought on by the fall, I'd have to say all of her major organs were healthy, including her heart, which would preclude any fainting or dizzy spells brought on by circulatory problems."

"Her family say she had no history of fainting or dizziness," Ryan put in, remembering his conversation with Kim's mother.

"In that case, let's turn to the more obvious injuries," Pinter said, and reached for a retractable pointer sitting on the desk. "Obviously, she sustained a number of nasty cuts and contusions as she broke through the glass window, but that's the least of it. She sustained severe blunt force trauma to the skull upon impact with the table. In fact, the impact was so severe, her nasal bone was pushed back into her brain matter. Look, here—"

"Howay, Jeff, it's Christmas," Phillips burst out.

"Sorry, sorry, I forget that other people aren't as fascinated by these things as I am." Pinter chuckled to himself, while the other two men tried not to think of skewered brains. "As for other injuries…well, where to begin? Her spleen and liver were ruptured, several ribs broken and fractured, which in turn pierced her left lung. Her spinal cord was damaged in several places but, aside from all that, you've got internal and external haemorrhaging on a massive scale."

They nodded, remembering a river of blood across the dining table.

"Ultimately there was what you might call 'polytrauma', because so many of her vital organs suffered catastrophic injury—the traumatic brain injuries would have been enough to do it, even without all the rest."

They were quiet for a moment as they looked upon the shell of what had once been a lovely young woman, her tanned skin now an ashen grey beneath the unforgiving light.

"What about defensive wounds?" Ryan asked.

"Again, nothing obvious," Pinter said. "The palms of her hands have a number of deep cuts, but we found shards of glass embedded in the skin, which could suggest she threw her hands out to prevent a fall…on the other hand, they might equally have been sustained on impact."

Pinter looked down at the body almost tenderly, as eager to help find the cause of her demise as they were, but his only source of information was the silent witness lying on the table before them.

"I'm waiting for the results of her nail swabs," he said. "Her clothing is going to take a while longer, too, but I can tell you that her nails could have been broken as she fell through the glass or fell on the table, just as easily as if she'd been in some sort of struggle. It doesn't help you much, but my bet would be that she was taken entirely by surprise and had very little time to react."

Ryan could imagine her fear, and it strengthened his resolve to find the person responsible.

"Was she sexually active?" he asked, though the fluffy handcuffs already suggested an answer to that question.

"Yes, and quite recently," Pinter said. "I'd say she had intercourse within hours of her death—I can also tell you that her partner wore a condom, because we found traces of spermicide on the walls of her vagina."

They stayed for another half an hour, but Pinter couldn't tell them anything further of interest until the laboratory returned the test results, so they thanked him and left him to his next case. They walked swiftly back along the hospital corridors, eager to put some distance between themselves and the underworld, and took a deep, nourishing breath of fresh air as they emerged onto the forecourt outside. By then, the sun had almost set, and the last of its rays burned a deep, fiery red, silhouetting the university and hospital buildings in that part of the city.

They made their way back to Ryan's car and only once they'd turned the heating onto full blast and availed themselves of the chair warmers did they reflect on Pinter's findings.

"At least we know she was unlikely to have fallen because of her own misadventure," Ryan said, referring to the term a coroner might use, should the case ever demand an inquest. "We also know there was a man involved, somewhere in all of this."

"Her family say she didn't have a boyfriend," Phillips said, with the kind of old-fashioned naivety that made him so downright lovable.

Ryan inclined his head. "No," he acknowledged. "But that doesn't mean she didn't have a casual relationship of some description. We already know she kept some sex toys beside her bed."

"Aye, well, my money's on that Doctor Quentin Jones," Phillips said. "He looks the type."

This last statement was said with such authority, Ryan could scarcely question its veracity.

Especially since it was entirely true.

"He does look the type," Ryan agreed. "You should've seen him turning on the charm for Charlie."

Phillips bristled with the kind of protectiveness he might have felt for his own daughter, if she were ever to face the unwanted attentions of a slimy predator. "The *nerve*!" he exclaimed. "I hope she booted him right up his bony arse—"

"I think he might have made a complaint on the grounds of disproportionate use of force, but I wouldn't have stopped her," Ryan said.

"Still, thinkin' of that poor lass lyin' dead in there, do you think there could have been an argument between them, and he decided he'd had enough? It would only have taken one hard push."

Ryan nodded. "Quentin's also her boss, so he could easily have fabricated some pretext to see her, even if it wasn't personal," he pointed out.

"That's interestin'," Phillips said. "What if she found somethin' valuable and he wanted to keep it for himself rather than put it on the archive sheet, as it were? A little bit of off-books income? It isn't as if the new owner would've known anythin' about it, would he?"

Ryan shook his head. "I can more easily believe that Jones would kill her for money than for any other reason," he said. "For a start, he isn't married, so there's nobody she'd threaten to speak to about any infidelity. He runs his own outfit, so there's no academic institution or HR department to complain to about anything."

"There's always the police, though."

"Exactly."

"Should we seize his mobile phone, bring him in?"

Ryan made a low sound of frustration. "Not enough to meet the threshold," he muttered. "We still can't prove she didn't stumble and fall, for a start. The cause of her death is entirely attributable to injuries sustained following a fall, and, unless Pinter tells us anything new, there's no evidence of third-party involvement. We don't have the grounds to take his personal effects."

"What if I ask him nicely?" Phillips wondered aloud.

"If you put on a dress and a pair of high heels, it might work."

That earned him a none-too-gentle punch in the arm.

CHAPTER 17

Ryan dropped his sergeant back at police headquarters and then took some personal time to high tail it back into the centre of town, where he was due to meet Anna for an appointment with a partner at one of the city's premier law firms—a specialist in intellectual property. The city was bustling for no apparent reason on a Monday afternoon, except that it was four days before Christmas and the streets were laden with market stalls touting food and drink, decorations, and knick-knacks of every description. The sweet scent of nutmeg and cinnamon carried on the air, along with a feeling of festive cheer Ryan hoped to enjoy, just as soon as their meeting was over.

Grey Street was an Edwardian feat of architecture, with its tall, delicately curved townhouses and columned grandeur of the Theatre Royal, running from the Earl Grey monument down towards Dean Street, which led on to the river. Ryan struggled to find a parking space nearby, so found himself power-walking through the crowd of ambling shoppers so as not to be late. However, as he passed the theatre, he spotted the sign for a forthcoming National Ballet performance of *The Nutcracker.* He checked the time on his watch and calculated that he had less than five minutes to dash into the box office and pick up some tickets, knowing that all three of the women in his life would love to see it.

He dashed inside.

Four and a half minutes later, Ryan re-emerged from the box office, a set of tickets safely tucked in his pocket.

Just then, he spotted Anna.

He stood on the steps outside the theatre and watched his wife—for the sheer pleasure of it. She was slightly taller than average, standing at five feet seven inches in her bare feet, but today she'd chosen a pair of smart suede knee boots with a bit of a heel, so her legs seemed even longer than usual as she moved elegantly through the crowds. She wore a tailored winter coat in a flattering shade of dark red that hugged her figure as well as keeping her warm in the frosty weather, while her dark hair fell in waves down her back, rippling as she walked briskly down the street towards their meeting point.

He was about to head over to join her, when her footsteps slowed and she began to look around, her eyes seeking something—

Him, Ryan realised.

Anna spotted him beneath the theatre's stone canopy, and her lips curved into a smile. Across the wide expanse of road, separated by the chattering heads of people jostling to find their favourite market stall, they found one another, and their eyes held.

The love he felt for her was fierce and uncompromising, and Ryan was struck by the very clear knowledge that he'd do almost anything for the woman he loved. For a man always in control, of himself and most situations he commanded, it was a disquieting thought.

Thrusting the thought aside, he jogged down the steps and across the street.

"Hello—" she said, before her mouth was captured in a deep kiss, and his arms wrapped around her, enfolding her against him, uncaring of the people passing by.

When they came up for air, she raised a gentle hand to stroke his face. "What was that for?" she whispered.

"Does there have to be a special reason to kiss you?" he asked, tucking a strand of hair behind her ear. "I saw you, and every primal instinct told me I should plant a smacker on your lips."

Anna giggled. "You've been spending too much time with Frank," she said.

"No doubt about that," he replied. "Just be glad I'm not taking any of his advice about what he calls The Art of Sweet Lovin'."

Anna smiled and shook her head. "I—"

"We should probably dash," he interrupted her. "Sorry, what were you going to say?"

"It can wait," she said, with a private smile. "Let's get this over with."

He took her hand, and they entered one of the buildings behind them which bore a shiny modern sign that declared it the offices of Simpson, Turner & Rosenberg.

Harold Rosenberg might have been slight of stature, but he was mighty in all other things.

The only child of Jewish refugees, he had been his parents' pride and joy. During the Second World War, his mother, Esther, had escaped across mainland Europe and on to the safer shores of England. She had been cared for by a family in the Lake District who'd taken the sixteen-year-old girl into their home with open hearts and minds, which was not always the case for those seeking asylum. Fear could be a terrible thing, Harold knew, and especially fear of the unknown.

In any event, his mother had met and married a young Jewish man and the pair had begun a new life together, resolving to make themselves as useful as possible to the community that had been so good to them. Abel had laboured until he could afford to buy his own small shop, where he made and repaired clocks and other timepieces, while Esther looked after their young son, Harold. By the time he'd finished school, the business had grown to such an extent that they could afford to send him to university.

Both of his parents were now dead, and had been for many years, but Harold had never forgotten the value of their hard work, nor their sense of fair play, which they'd instilled in him from an early age. Aside from repairs and construction, his father had also designed beautiful clocks and watches. One day, Abel had seen one of his designs replicated in the window of a smart jewellers on the other side of town. The battle that ensued to claim his workmanship had brought with it a flurry of anti-Semitic abuse, and, in the end, Abel Rosenberg had chosen the path of least resistance. He knew the value of peace, after all, and had no desire to stir up bad feeling amongst those who would only say he was being greedy, or telling lies.

But he never designed anything else after that.

Harold had never forgotten the dejected look on his father's face, nor the injustice of it all, and that abiding feeling had carried him through his legal training and into a successful career helping other creative people to protect what was rightfully theirs.

He awaited one of them now.

"Mr Rosenberg? Your three-thirty has arrived."

"Thank you, Irene, show them in would you, please?"

A moment later, there was a knock on the door of his office and in stepped one of the most handsome couples he'd ever seen outside the pages of *Tatler* magazine.

"Ah, Mr Finley-Ryan, Doctor Taylor-Ryan, please do take a seat."

Ryan and Anna accepted cups of very fine ground coffee, and only when the outer door closed behind Rosenberg's secretary did they get down to the matter at hand.

"So," Harold said, clasping his hands together. "I understand you're having some trouble in the world of publishing?" He looked between them, unsure of whom he should address.

"I arranged this meeting, Mr Rosenberg, but it's on behalf of my wife," Ryan said, shifting his body to make it clear she was in charge of proceedings.

"I see," he murmured. "And what can I help you with, Mrs Ryan?"

It was a natural slip, and one Anna readily forgave. She might have kept part of her own name, and have quite a few letters after it, but she was an unpretentious woman who was never offended by a lack of formality.

"Please, call me Anna," she said, and the man smiled, his face crinkling like an accordion. "Well, I'm an academic historian by profession, and have a position at Durham University where I still work part-time as a lecturer and supervising postgraduate and doctoral students."

He nodded, encouraging her to continue.

"Over the past few years, I started to think about writing fiction, for a change," she said. "I was born on Holy Island, and…let's say, we've had some interesting experiences there—"

"You can say that, again," Ryan put in, to make her smile.

"—which inspired me to write a kind of supernatural murder mystery set on the island."

"Sounds great," the solicitor said. "What's the fly in the ointment?"

She gave him a pained smile. "I wrote the manuscript, tinkered with it, and had it in the best shape I could make it," she said. "I made the mistake of attending a creative writing session, last year. Oh, there's nothing wrong with that, in principle," she hastened to add. "Unfortunately, the leader of this group is a writer themselves, and—well, you probably won't believe this, but—"

"I will believe people capable of almost anything," Harold murmured. "In fact, let me guess. This writer stole your work, and has published it themselves?"

To her embarrassment, tears burned at the back of Anna's eyes, and she nodded. "Yes," she said softly. "We only discovered this had happened very recently, almost by chance. I wouldn't have known until I'd seen the book on a shelf in a bookshop, otherwise."

Harold nodded, his lips flattening into a hard line. "Tell me, Anna, how do you think this person—what's their name?"

"Her professional name is Lin Oldman," Anna said.

Harold raised an eyebrow, having recognised the name immediately. "All right," he said. "How do you think she might have been able to copy your work? It's worth mentioning, at this stage, how common it is for writers to craft very similar stories without ever having met one another, or without any malicious intention."

Ryan opened his mouth, then clamped it shut again, determined to allow Anna to be her own advocate.

"I understand that," she said. "However, having read a sample, it's clear the wording has simply been changed, here and there. She's changed a few of the character names, too, but everything else is identical. As for how it could have happened, I suppose that's my fault—"

"It isn't your fault," Ryan couldn't help but say. "You can't blame yourself for someone else's duplicitousness."

She nodded, and took the hand he offered, cradling it between her own for support. "I—I took a hard copy of my manuscript along to the creative writing session and I must have been tired or distracted, because I ended up leaving it behind. I rang the library when I got home, to ask if anything had been handed in, but they said they couldn't find anything matching its description. I assumed the cleaning team had binned it, or somebody had picked it up by mistake…I don't know. In any case, I never imagined this would happen."

"Nobody ever does," Harold said, and proceeded to ask a few more questions, which Anna answered as honestly as she could.

"Well?" Ryan asked him, once the interrogation was over. "What's your view on the matter?"

Harold wished he had better news for the nice, honest couple seated before him. However, as his grandparents could readily have attested, sometimes, life just wasn't fair.

"Essentially, we are talking about plagiarism, which is the act of taking someone else's work or ideas and passing them off as one's own without crediting the owner of that intellectual property," he said, so he could be sure they were all reading from the same hymn sheet. "This can take various forms...copying content verbatim, paraphrasing or borrowing phrases and ideas from various sources and putting them all together. The question is whether it would constitute a legally actionable copyright infringement."

They nodded.

"Now, this is where things can get sticky," he warned them. "It isn't possible to have copyright in an idea for a story, but rather in how an idea is *expressed*. To that end, we look at linguistic formation, choice of words, themes, arguments and so forth. Now, in cases of commercial fiction, storylines do tend to reflect similar themes, sometimes—"

He went on to explain how difficult it may be to prove that the themes Anna had employed in her manuscript were unique, but these things were decided on a case-by-case basis.

"The next step is to conduct a thorough examination of both texts, but it's also worth mentioning that Ms Oldman will undoubtedly receive the protection of her publisher, should any litigation arise," he said, meaningfully. "I know that the urge to have one's 'day in court' can be overwhelming, at times, but I would caution you to consider the wider reputational implications. The world of publishing is a smaller one than you think. I don't say this because I disbelieve the truth of the matter, but because it's sometimes a question of cost-benefit analysis."

It would go against every natural instinct to do nothing, Ryan thought, but it would be Anna's decision to make.

"What are the next steps?" he asked.

"That would be for me to have a thorough read-through of both documents, so I can look at the material and see the similarities for myself."

They talked a while longer, listening to Rosenberg's detailed explanation of what would be worth litigating, examples of cases that had been won and lost, and felt that he was, at least, everything they had hoped he would be. An hour later, they thanked him, and Ryan took Anna's hand as they made their way back outside. They discussed the solicitor's well-intentioned advice but, just as Anna was on the cusp of telling Ryan she'd rather not bother wasting their time in litigation, they happened to pass by the window of a large bookseller on their way back to her car.

There, on display, was Lin Oldman's new book.

Her book, Anna thought, and her spine stiffened.

There was always something to be done.

CHAPTER 18

Ryan's team gathered at police headquarters ahead of a briefing at five o'clock. While they awaited the man himself, they fortified themselves with caffeine and, in Phillips' case, used up his daily sugar allowance in ordering a sticky bun from the staff canteen.

"Hi Charlie," Mel said, entering the break room to find her new colleague spooning coffee into several mugs.

"Hi Mel!" Charlie replied, in a voice that was a touch over-bright. "Would you like one of these?"

"Oh, that's kind of you...white, one sugar, please."

Charlie nodded, and splashed some milk into another mug, stirring in a teaspoon of sugar while Mel rooted out a tin of biscuits.

"I think they were moved into the top cupboard," Charlie murmured. "To help Frank help himself, Denise said."

Sure enough, Mel found a half-full tin of Marks & Spencer's finest offerings hidden in the uppermost cupboard. "Bingo," she said, making a grab for them. "Things have changed a bit around here, if there's a biscuit to be had. I remember a time when you'd need to keep them under lock and key."

Charlie didn't look up, and focused all her attention on pouring hot water into six mugs.

"Frank's been doing well, keeping to his diet," she said, and began lifting the mugs onto a wooden tray.

"Actually, better make that seven," Mel said. "I think Faulkner was hoping to pop in and give us an update."

Charlie nodded and added another mug. There was a long pause while neither woman spoke, instead listening to the everyday sounds of water hitting porcelain and pigeons cooing on the window ledge outside. Mel watched Charlie's hands as they worked and found herself saying more than she meant to.

"Tom's a great guy, you know," she said, and wondered why she sounded so desperate to convince her of it. "He was married, years ago, but he's a steady person with a kind heart."

Charlie murmured something in polite agreement.

"Jack was only saying this morning, he thinks the two of you would be a great match, actually."

Charlie's hand stilled, as the words circled her mind. "Did he?" she said, softly. "Well, we can't all be as lucky in love as the two of you."

She lifted the tray and, when she turned around, her face was unreadable. "Shall we go?"

Mel nodded, and followed Charlie towards the conference room, feeling something niggle at the lining of her stomach. Something that might have been guilt.

Then again, it was true what they said.

All's fair in love and war.

"Here," she said. "Let me get the door for you."

Charlie entered the conference room to a chorus of thanks from the others already seated at the long table.

"That's the ticket," Denise said, as the hot liquid warmed her belly. "Ryan better get here soon, otherwise I'll have to dash off to pick Samantha up from her friend's house."

"He's on his way," Jack said, having already received a message to that effect. "Charlie, are you okay for time? I know your mum has Ben—"

"I'm fine, thanks." The reply was entirely cordial but lacked its usual warmth.

Jack frowned, but then the door opened again to admit Ryan, with Faulkner in tow.

"Look who I found, loitering with intent," he said, reaching for one of the mugs.

"Do you mind if I sit here?" Tom asked Charlie, indicating the chair next to hers.

"Not at all," she said, and directed a brief, fulminating glare in Jack's direction.

Pink-eared, Faulkner took up the space and sipped his own coffee, to give his hands something to do.

"Right then," Ryan said. "Let's get down to it...*Frank*?"

Phillips held up a hand. "Not now, son. I'm havin' a moment."

Ryan folded his arms across his chest, and tipped back in his chair. "Are we disturbing you?"

"Aye," came the honest reply, between mouthfuls of sticky bun. "This is the highlight of my day, so there'll be no talk o' murder until it's finished."

If she hadn't been possessed of such a good sense of humour, his wife might have taken issue with the fact that he'd described a sticky bun as the highlight rather than anything else she might care to mention but, as it was, she merely shook her head.

A moment later, he licked the last of the icing from his fingertips, dabbed his lips with a paper napkin, and then clapped his hands together. "Reet!" he said. "Let's talk about murder."

"Well, if you're *quite* ready," Ryan said. "Let's start with Kimberley Foster. I take it there's no need to recap the details, considering we were all in attendance, but the upshot is, we have a twenty-five-year-old woman whose death was confirmed as being the result of polytrauma. That is to say, multiple serious injuries to her vital organs after a fall of more than thirty feet."

"Pinter's confirmed it, then?" Charlie asked, and Ryan nodded.

"He'll send us his written report as soon as the toxicology and blood tests come back, but he's examined her body and, prior to the fall, she was a young woman in the best of health. I spoke with her family yesterday, and again this morning, to ask about previous medical history, but they weren't aware of any psychological or physical problems she might have been having. I've requested the medical records from her GP surgery, which is based in Lancashire, where Kimberley was from. I anticipate they'll corroborate what her family already believe to have been the case."

"Her friends said the same, and so did the estate staff," Charlie put in. "They all described Kimberley as cheerful, and not the type to have committed suicide."

"Sabrina said much the same," Ryan added. "For his part, her boss, Quentin Jones, could offer no reason she might have had to be unhappy or, worse still, suicidal."

Ryan paused to swig more coffee before continuing.

"We've requested her bank account data, which we're waiting to receive, and her mobile phone records directly from the provider—which took some time to ascertain, considering her phone is still missing, as is her laptop computer. They're both Apple devices, so I've asked digital forensics to see if they can track their whereabouts, but we can safely assume someone didn't want us to find whatever might be on the digital record." Ryan flashed a smile. "Which is all the more reason for us to find them," he finished. "Now, it's worth saying that, if it wasn't for the disappearance of these items, we'd have very little to suggest that Kimberley's death was suspicious. As it is, we have to ask ourselves who might have had the means, the motive and the opportunity to push her through that window—because that's the most likely way she came down."

Ryan drew back his chair and picked up a whiteboard marker, to begin writing down the names of key people on site at the time of her death.

"All staff who were present at the dinner last night have already been contacted for their statements," he began. "I'm not ruling anything out, but, for the sake of discussion, I'm going to discount the involvement of any police personnel, for the time being. That leaves us with the catering staff belonging to an outside company, rather than the usual team who operate the tearoom during the day. Five Star Catering & Events supplied and served dinner, which included the waiting staff. In total, there were eleven of them, including an on-site chef and two sous chefs. They've all been interviewed, but nothing flagged as unusual, and none of them admit any acquaintance with the deceased."

Next, Ryan wrote a column headed 'ESTATE STAFF' and turned back to his team.

"Several of the hall's permanent staff occupy cottages on the estate, some quite close to the hall itself, and others within a walking distance," he said, and began listing the names of those with tenanted properties. "There are farmers and ground staff; gardeners, including Daisy Flowers, her son Henry and her mother, Linda; the head gardener, Paul Bullman; the acting estate manager, Adrian, and his wife, Carol—"

He listed some other names, all of whom worked on the estate and lived within its boundary walls.

"In terms of staff who don't live on-site, but were present last night, we've got Barbara Elder, the events manager, Lesley, Susan, Michelle, Beverley and Ged. They work at the hall during the day and occasionally help out with events, which is still a fairly new venture for them, so they all muck in together."

"When we interviewed them, they all said they knew Kimberley, but not well," Denise put in. "They described her as friendly, but said she kept herself to herself."

"That Daisy Flowers lass seemed to think she was a bit out of sorts, a day or two before she died," Frank pointed out. "So far, she's the only one who noticed."

"Did she happen to mention why?" Ryan asked.

"No such luck," Frank replied. "That'd be too easy, wouldn't it?"

Ryan smiled, and turned back to the whiteboard.

"Then, there are her conservation colleagues," he said, and wrote 'CONSERVATION TEAM' in block capitals at the top of a fresh column of names. "Charlie and I interviewed Sabrina Fisher, who's compiling a written history of Belsay Hall and Estate, and her boss as well as Kimberley's boss, Doctor Quentin Jones. He's what I believe you, Frank, would describe as being a 'reet poser', in every sense of the word, and has a taste for the finer things in life, which includes the young women he employs."

"Has he got caps on his teeth?" Frank queried.

"Definitely," Charlie replied.

"Year-round tan?"

She nodded again.

"Lots of prominent labels on his clothes, giant watch, wanker car?"

"Yes, to all of the above."

"Aye, you've got a garden variety poser there," he confirmed, as though she'd described the symptoms of a common cold. "Now, if y'ask me, the problem with these middle-aged blokes nowadays is that they're chasin' the past. Now, take me, a man in peak physical shape—"

MacKenzie gave him a sidelong glance.

"—you don't catch me hoppin' on a Ryanair flight and comin' back a week later, lookin' like a wally—"

"I could remind you of that trip to Dublin, last Paddy's Day," Jack put in.

"That was *entirely* different—" Phillips began.

"This is all very interesting," Ryan interjected. "But is there a point, Frank?"

"Look, all I'm sayin' is, there's some who like the younger lasses because they don't give them any trouble," he said. "They haven't lived enough of life to know any better, so they're easily impressed. Sounds like this Quentin Whatjermacallhim is one of those. He likes to have his ego flattered by pretty young women and, since he's also the boss, they probably feel some sort of pressure to behave themselves, or else lose their jobs."

"Go on," Ryan said.

"We know from chattin' with Pinter that the lass—Kimberley, that is—was sexually active," Phillips continued. "In fact, he seems to think she had a bit of it on the day she died. Now, if she was with someone besides her boss, who's still the number one suspect on my list, it could've been a married man—"

"Like Adrian?" Mel suggested, and he nodded.

"Aye, like him, or one of the other tenants," Phillips said, eyeing Ryan's list on the whiteboard. "She might've been puttin' pressure on him to leave his wife, or many a thing."

"It's a good theory, but it's conjecture at the moment," Ryan decided. "Until we have those telephone, medical and account records, we still have an absence of motive or evidence. Tom? Can you tell us anything useful about the scene?"

Faulkner came to attention and, in doing so, brushed Charlie's arm.

He turned red.

"Sorry," he muttered, and tried to unscramble his thoughts. "Um, well, the team spent hours last night and all of today going over the main site at Belsay. That includes the area around the broken window and the flat roof surrounding it, the access points inside that part of the house and up to the attic, and the immediate vicinity surrounding the house to try to determine if anyone had entered or left the property by a window or some other means."

"And did you find anything?" Ryan asked him.

Faulkner pulled an apologetic face. "Sorry to say, we didn't," he replied. "Aside from existing tracks in the snow, we found no evidence of any footprints leading off across the fields. That being said, we weren't able to cover the whole area in such a short space of time, at night and with a limited team. By this morning, most of the snow had melted away to slush, which didn't help."

It was only what Ryan had suspected, but it was still disappointing not to hear of a neat trail of size-ten walking boots leading from the hall to the front door of one of the tenant cottages.

"Anything else?" he asked.

"We swabbed the whole area and combed around for trace samples," Faulkner told him. "I'm waiting for the lab to return the results but, the simple answer, is 'no'. There was no bloodshed visible to the naked eye, no torn clothing or other handy articles to suggest anyone had ever been up on the roof before Kimberley fell. The door handles had no prints on them—"

Ryan looked up at that.

"None whatsoever?" he said, and Faulkner shook his head.

"None, other than some prints on the outer door leading to the servants' quarters and up to the attics," he said. "They match Adrian's."

"He opened the outer door to give us access, last night," Charlie reminded them.

"I still don't understand how the door out onto the roof was entirely clean of prints," Ryan persisted. "Unless—"

Of course.

"He or she wiped them, before they left."

Faulkner nodded. "It's all I can think."

"Not very bright, are they?" Mel remarked. "It's always going to be a red flag for the police to find no prints, not even old ones, on a handle that's in regular use."

They nodded in agreement.

"It's possible they pushed her without intending to kill, and had to think on the fly," Jack said. "They would've been panicking, so they're bound to make silly mistakes."

"Even in cases of premeditated murder, people panic," Denise said. "These jokers always think they've covered every base."

"Kimberley's clothing is being analysed, and swabs we took from her body are being processed now by Pinter's team," Faulkner went on to say. "It's possible we may get lucky and find some errant hair on her jacket, but I've already told you there were no signs of a struggle, and the wounds on her body were entirely consistent with a traumatic fall rather than any kind of altercation. I don't think this will turn out to be one where the DNA evidence leads you to their front door, more's the pity."

Ryan stuck his hands in his pockets and looked at the clock on the wall. "Before we call it a night, then, let's have a quick update on those human remains down at North Shields," he said, turning to Jack and Mel. "Any ID?"

Jack shook his head. "Not yet," he said. "More body parts washed up while we were at the scene, so they've all been transferred for assessment and to see whether they belong to the same person."

"It's a start," Ryan agreed, with a smile.

"It might take a while to positively ID the person," Mel said. "For one thing, the parts were semi-decomposed and bloated by the water, so any facial features were entirely unrecognisable for identity purposes. There were no teeth inside the head, and no clothing or other personal effects to be found, although the dive team are going to head back and trawl the river again to see if they can find more. On the face of it, somebody went to a lot of trouble to make sure this person wasn't found and, if he was, that it would be difficult to name him."

Ryan nodded. "A gangland murder, you reckon?"

"That's what we're thinking," Jack agreed. "The cuts to the torso were professional, done almost surgically, or by someone with plenty of experience. It looks like a professional job, or one done by a clinical professional, at least."

"All right," Ryan said. "Keep digging and see what turns up—no pun intended. See if there are any potential matches to Missing Persons and have a word with our informants and see if they've heard anything on the street."

Jack and Mel gave their agreement, and soon after, the team disbanded. Before she could run off, Faulkner took his life in his hands and asked Charlie the question he'd been wanting to ask her for weeks.

"Charlie—um, before you go—"

She paused briefly in the act of tugging on her coat. "Yep?"

"Ah, well, I was wondering—if—if—"

She waited, trying not to look at the clock again. "Yes?"

Tom cleared a constriction in his throat and tried again. "I wonder if you'd let me take you out—to dinner, or—or, a movie, sometime?"

His throat wobbled, and Charlie stared at him for long seconds, wondering if Jack had also spoken with his friend and put him up to it.

Either way, it was clear where his interest lay, and it was certainly not with her.

She caught his eye across the room, then looked away again.

"That would be lovely, Tom, thank you for asking," she said, and gave him a blinding smile. "What are you doing, this Friday?"

"Friday?" he squeaked. "N—nothing. I'm doing nothing. That is, if you want, we can have dinner then. That would be—good."

He almost slapped a palm to his own face, and wondered if she now thought he was a simpleton.

"It's a date," she said, raising her voice slightly so it could be heard across the room. "Here, let me give you my number."

Jack watched as Charlie scribbled her digits onto the back of a scrap of paper, and Faulkner folded it carefully before tucking the number inside his trouser pocket. He liked Tom Faulkner, and always had. But, in that moment, he felt murderous.

"Jack? Shall we make a move?"

He looked sharply at Mel, and wondered if she was reading his mind.

When he looked back, it was to find that Charlie and Tom had already left, chatting happily as they made their way down the corridor.

CHAPTER 19

When Ryan arrived back at the house in Bamburgh, he was greeted by the thundering paws of a girl of three and a golden Labrador puppy, both of whom raced across the hall to pounce upon him as he came through the front door.

"Daddy!"

Ryan caught Emma up into his arms, noting belatedly that her dungarees were covered in flour and other mysterious substances which had, undoubtedly, transferred themselves onto his white shirt.

His *formerly* white shirt.

Ryan held her tight, enjoying the warmth of his daughter's embrace, and then she wriggled away again, clattering back towards the kitchen to inform her mother and grandmother that he was home. Before heading through to join them, Ryan petted the dog, who presented his furry belly for a good scratch, and procured a small dog treat from his jacket pocket.

"*Rascal*!" his daughter bellowed, her young voice echoing around the walls.

The puppy scrambled to his feet and lolloped away.

"Another disciple," he said to himself, and hung his coat on the peg beside the door before trailing after her, too.

Entering the kitchen, he found his mother stirring curry powder into a pan of simmering chicken, and she offered him her cheek.

"Hello, dear," she said. "How was your day?"

"Not bad," he said, snaffling a piece of naan bread fresh from the oven. "Where's Anna?"

"She's having a lie down," his mother said.

Instantly, he was concerned. "Was it the meeting with the solicitor?" he wondered aloud. "I thought she didn't seem herself, afterwards—"

"Why don't you go and check on her?" Eve suggested, realising that Anna mustn't have found the right moment to tell him her news.

Ryan took her advice and, when Emma would have followed him, her grandmother held her back under the pretence of helping to lay the table for dinner.

"They'll be down in a moment," she said. "Now, where do the forks go?"

Ryan stuck his head around the door to the master bedroom, where he found Anna curled up on top of the bed with an empty bucket on the floor beside her.

"Only me," he said, and came to sit on the bed beside her.

Anna began to get up, but he stopped her.

"I'll come to you," he said, and kicked off his shoes so that he could curl up beside her. "Are you feeling unwell?"

Anna put her hand over his, and rested her head back against his chest, where she heard the strong rhythm of his heart. "I wouldn't quite say that," she replied. "I feel very sickly, from time-to-time, but otherwise I'm well. Very well, in fact."

The penny still didn't drop.

"Do you think it's a stomach bug, or something you ate?" he asked. "It could be the stress of the day, catching up with you—"

"I don't think it's any of those things," she said, and turned around in his arms so that she could look at him. "In fact, I'm pretty sure I know the ailment."

His eyes were a brilliant, silvery blue as they searched her face for answers.

Then, all of a sudden, he began to smile.

"You're not—?"

"Pregnant?" she said, and nodded. "Yes, I am."

The smile lit up his whole face. "Anna, this is wonderful news," he said, reverently, and cradled her in his arms. "Are you happy, darling?"

"I'm nervous, scared and not looking forward to nine months of waddling around," she said, with a smile.

"But I'm also very, very happy. I wonder if we'll have a boy, or another little girl."

"Do you mind?"

"Not a bit," she said. "So long as the baby's healthy, that's all I care about."

He looked down at her stomach, which was still flat, and placed a hand gently against it before lowering his head to kiss her skin beneath the jumper she wore.

"I love you," he said, and kissed her thoroughly. "What can I do? Do you need—what was it, the last time? Crackers and ginger beer?"

She pulled a horrified face. "Eugh," she said. "I couldn't face either of those…but I could go for some tomatoes and lemon meringue pie?"

"Well, that makes total sense," he said, and she swatted his arm.

"It's not my fault," she said, sweetly. "It's what the baby needs."

"The baby needs *pudding*?" he said, disbelievingly. "Are you sure this isn't Frank's love child you're carrying?"

They both laughed, and then rolled off the bed to join the family downstairs. Before she could make her way down the stairs, Ryan took her hand in his.

"I can't wait for this next adventure," he said.

"Well, you've got that right," she said. "You've met our daughter, haven't you?"

She thought she saw a ripple of panic, quickly disguised. "It'll be fine," he said. "How hard can it be, looking after two rather than one?"

Neither of them decided to answer that question, being fully aware that ignorance was bliss.

"Should we tell Emma?"

"Let's wait a while longer," Anna decided. "Just until we can be more secure in the pregnancy. Maybe after the four-month mark?"

"How far along are you?" he asked.

"I think about a month, but I've got an appointment with the doctor tomorrow, so I'll have a better idea after they've checked things over."

Ryan smiled again. "We'd better hurry up and finish this renovation, eh? We need to kit out a nursery."

"Maybe, this time, you can hire a handyman to put the cot up," she said. "It was painful to watch, the last time."

"Duly noted."

"Looks like Tom plucked up the courage to ask Charlie out."

Mel watched as Jack chopped tofu into a wok of sizzling vegetables, having refused any help with the food preparation.

"Yeah," was all he could think to say, and kept his back turned as he stirred their food.

"They're both nice people," Mel continued. "I hope it works out for them."

Jack nodded, and reached for a bowl of oriental seasoning, which he sprinkled over the pan.

"I know you must have been…lonely, while I was gone," Mel said, carefully. "Did you see anyone, while we were apart? I wouldn't blame you, if you had."

Jack turned the heat down and reached for a couple of plates. "No, I didn't see anyone," he said.

He didn't ask whether she had, but Melanie answered the question, anyway.

"I talked to a few people," she said. "Had a drink here and there, but nothing physical. They weren't you."

At another time, they were words he'd have been delighted to hear, but, this time, he found he was unmoved.

"Why did you come back, Mel?" he asked her, suddenly. "Was it for me, or the job?"

She was taken aback. "W-what do you mean? I came back for you, of course."

He said nothing, so she carried on.

"I mean, of course I love my work, but so do you," she said. "There's no harm in coming back for both, is there?"

Jack shook his head.

"I haven't changed," Melanie said, quietly. "I might have a bit of a tan, and I might have worked through some PTSD, but I'm still the same person I was before I left. I want to travel more but, this time, with you beside me.

I'll get married, if you want to, but I'm not fussed, either way. I don't particularly want children, but I'll have them if it will make you happy."

He turned off the hob, and placed a bowl of stir-fried tofu and vegetables in front of her.

"Jack?"

When he met her eyes, his own were filled with sadness. "You might not have changed, but I think I have," he said, as gently as he could. "But, in some things, I haven't changed at all. I've always wanted a home, and a family together with someone I love. I'm a homebody, at heart, no matter what you might think. I want to put down roots, Mel, not tear them up and travel the world. I'm happy with my own company, nowadays, and I like children. I know you say you'd have them to make me happy, but that wouldn't make *you* happy, and it wouldn't be fair to them, anyway."

She couldn't argue with that, for it was only the truth. "Yes," she said, as tears pooled in her eyes. "I left it too late to come home, didn't I?"

Jack sat down on one of the bar stools beside her. "You took as long as you needed to recover, which means it was exactly the right amount of time," he replied, and gave her hand a squeeze. "I love you and care for you, Mel, and I'm grateful for all the time we've had together. But we want different things, now. I think, if we're really, truly honest with ourselves, we've always wanted slightly different things, and there's nothing wrong with that."

A tear ran down her cheek, and she dashed it away. "It's Charlie, isn't it?" she said. "You've fallen for her."

He didn't like to tell lies, so he simply nodded. "Yes, I think I have. I'm sorry, I never meant to."

Melanie wanted to be angry with him, to feel hurt by the emotional betrayal, but he hadn't done anything wrong. In fact, he'd acted honourably, from beginning to end.

"Thank you," she said, and, this time, she gave his hand a squeeze. "Thank you for being honest with me, and for choosing to finish one relationship before trying to start another. Not everybody has the courage to do it the right way."

He nodded.

"Jack, I—" She looked down at her plate, and told herself to be as honest as he had. "I had a feeling you liked Charlie, and, I suppose, I was jealous. When I was speaking to her, earlier today, I might have suggested that you thought it was a good idea she give Tom Faulkner a chance."

Jack sighed. *That would explain the chilly reception,* he thought. Charlie believed he felt nothing for her, and had even discussed her love life with his partner, like a pair of matchmakers. "Thanks for telling me," he said, once he'd overcome the initial wave of frustration. "That can't have been easy to say, either."

"Thank you for looking after me, during the worst time of my life," she said. "I'll never forget it, Jack. You're a good man, and I hope Charlie sees that, some day."

"You've been there for me, too," he said. "Thank you for believing in me, when I stopped believing in myself."

They smiled at one another, through the tears, and then held each other in a long, caring embrace.

"Love you," he mumbled.

"You too," she replied. "I'll always be your friend, if you need me."

"Same goes, Yates. Same goes."

CHAPTER 20

The next day

The skies were still a deep, midnight blue when Ryan awakened the following morning. It was not his alarm clock that had broken his sleep, nor any circadian rhythm, but the feeling once again of being watched.

"I know you're watching me, again," he mumbled.

"No, I'm not," Emma whispered, and he smiled at her blatant subterfuge.

"Tell me something, kid. Why don't you ever spy on your mummy while she sleeps?"

"I do," she said, blithely. "But you're funnier."

Ryan didn't know what to think about that.

Funnier?

"I'm not a funny sleeper," he said, and was almost certain it was true.

"Your eyebrows wiggle," she said, pointing at the slashes of black hair above his blue eyes. "You're like Rascal, because his face twitches in his sleep, too."

Now, he was like the puppy, Ryan thought.

Brilliant.

"For one thing, only the most wise and intelligent of daddies have wiggly eyebrows," he said, reaching to lift her onto the bed so she could find her favourite place between the pair of them.

If Emma thought that was a load of nonsense, she said nothing of it, and let him believe he had her fooled.

"Is grandma going to stay with us?" she asked instead.

"Just a little while longer," Ryan replied. "Remember, she has her own home to go to, but we'll visit her as often as we can."

A moment later, the pooch burst into the room, seeking a bit of the snuggle action.

"Oi!" Ryan said. "Off the bed!"

The puppy put its paws on his chest, tail wagging happily.

From beneath the covers, he thought he heard a snigger from his wife.

"I heard that," he said, and Anna turned over to smile at him and the dog, who was receiving a thorough tickle between the ears.

"I thought you said dogs respected their master's tone of command?" she said.

"He does," Ryan said, and looked the puppy straight in its big, chocolate brown eyes. "Rascal? Off the bed!"

The dog merely licked his chin.

"Yes, I see what you mean," Anna said, and Emma giggled.

"All right, smarty-pants, I bet he doesn't do it for you, either," Ryan said, and felt a prescient fear that he'd just uttered words he'd live to regret.

"What do I win, if you lose?"

"Breakfast in bed?"

"Done," Anna said, and levered herself upwards, ignoring the pang of nausea that rocketed through her system in order to face the little dog.

She looked at him and raised a finger. "Rascal? Off the bed, now!"

Ryan watched the dog jump neatly down from the bed and sit on the floor, where he waited to be praised, tail wagging.

"I don't believe it," he said. "What are you, some sort of sorceress?"

"When it comes to big, daft things," Anna teased, and planted a kiss on his lips. "Now, Emma and I will have toast with jam, please."

"I'm a slave to these women," Ryan said to the dog. "C'mon, you traitor, I'll get you a treat while I'm looking for the jam."

An hour later, Ryan was on the motorway heading south towards police headquarters when a call came through from Frank, which he answered using the hands-free system.

"What's up?" he said to the disembodied voice at the other end of the line. "You miss me so much you couldn't wait until I got to the office, or what?"

"Har har," Phillips said, and Ryan swiftly turned down the volume as his sergeant's booming voice almost jolted the car off the road. "It's the gardener, Daisy Flowers, from Belsay Hall. Turns out, she rang and left a message with the switchboard, but they forgot to pass it on."

"Great," Ryan said, mildly. "Was it important?"

"Maybe," Phillips said. "Daisy remembered that she overheard an argument between Kimberley and the head gardener, Paul Bullman, the day before she died. Apparently, he'd used some antique wood and whatnot, to build himself a rack for his gardening tools. She booted off about it, when she found out, and threatened to tell the new owner all about it. Daisy didn't give it another thought, really, except that they were really going at it, and, at one point, Bullman said something like, *if you tell anyone about this, it'll be the last thing you do around here.*"

"Well, that's not very nice," Ryan said. "I think we should have a word with Mr Bullman, don't you, Frank?"

"My thoughts, entirely," came the reply. "I'll see you there."

When Ryan and Phillips arrived at Belsay Hall, it was to find that Paul Bullman was missing.

"He isn't in the farmhouse," Phillips said. "Any luck at the hall?"

Ryan shook his head.

"Nobody's seen him all morning," he replied, feeling a prickle beginning to spread along the base of his spine. "Knock on all the doors again, and ask to look around if they'll let you do it without a warrant. I'll ask the estate staff to help me search the outbuildings."

Two hours passed by, during which time they performed an exhaustive search of the hall, its formal grounds and the many outbuildings dotted around the estate. When they reconvened in the courtyard café, which, to Phillips' dismay, still offered warm scones to the passing traveller, it was only to declare that nobody had been able to locate the head gardener.

"His phone is turned off," Adrian said, worriedly. "You don't think he's responsible for Kimberley's death, do you?"

Ryan didn't reply, but instead turned to Phillips and spoke in an undertone.

"Put out an APW," he said. "I want everyone to be on the lookout for a man matching his description."

Phillips nodded, and left the room, while Ryan turned to face the small crowd of staff gathered before him.

"I know it can be difficult to imagine one of your friends or colleagues being involved in anything untoward," he said, in as stern a voice he could muster for a Tuesday morning. "However, you have to put personal feelings aside and remember that we're here to find out how Kimberley Foster met her tragic death. She has a family who loved her, and a life she could have led."

He paused to let those words sink in.

"If *any* of you having anything else you think I should know, now's the time to tell me," he said, looking between them.

They looked back at him.

"Well, it was worth a try," he muttered, and swore as his phone began to bleat in his pocket.

Morrison.

That was all he needed.

"Chief?" he said, walking to a quiet corner of the café.

"Ryan, I don't know if you realise, but it's Christmas," she said, straight off the bat.

"I had noticed, ma'am."

"Had you? That's good, because I was beginning to wonder, considering I've just approved an APW for a man named Paul Bullman, who's reportedly absconded from his home and workplace at Belsay Hall. Is that correct?"

"Yes, as far as we know."

"I see," she replied. "Was the nationwide manhunt we conducted over the past few months not satisfying enough for you, or were you missing the added excitement and felt that we needed to begin another?"

"Neither," he replied. "Trouble just seems to find me, I suppose."

"Don't get cute, Ryan."

"Sorry."

At the other end of the line, the Chief Constable sighed audibly.

"Look, I've got nice plans for Christmas day," she told him. "So should you. Let's get this wrapped up and tied in a pretty red bow with bells on, before Santa Claus comes down the chimney. Okay?"

"We're doing all we can."

She rang off, and Ryan headed back outside to perform a final check of the farmhouse, in case they'd missed any clues as to Bullman's whereabouts, the first time around. As he was crossing the driveway, he ran into Mark Newman, who'd recently returned from opening the Christmas fete at the local primary school.

"Back again, Chief Inspector?" he said. "Have you found out what happened to Kimberley?"

"We're investigating all leads," Ryan replied, using the standard line. "Have you seen Paul Bullman today?"

Newman thought about it, then shook his head. "No, I'm afraid I haven't seen him since yesterday," he said. "Is something the matter?"

Ryan didn't reply to that, and started to make for the farmhouse when Newman made a small sound of surprise in the back of his throat.

"The clock's wrong," he said.

"Sorry?"

"The clock," Newman said, pointing up at the large clock at the top of a tall stone tower. "It's wrong."

"No sign of Bullman in the quarry garden," Adrian declared, making his way across the gravel from the direction of the estate's spectacular exotic garden that had grown up from blasted rock to create a vision of flora and fauna. "What did you say was wrong?"

Perhaps he should have addressed Newman by his formal title, as baronet, Adrian thought. On the other hand, it only gave the upper classes ideas above their station, in his view.

"The clock in the tower over there," Newman said, again. "It seems to have stopped."

Ryan and Adrian turned to look up at the clock, then at their own watches.

"You're right," Adrian said, with a touch of professional embarrassment. "That's strange, because I set it and wound the mechanism last Friday, same as always. Let me go and see if there's a fault."

"I don't think we've looked in the clock tower yet," Ryan said. "I'll come with you."

The clock tower was like much of the rest of Belsay, which is to say it was old and dusty, but brimming with charm. Adrian unlocked the door using the master key he kept in the safe beside his desk and the three men stepped inside and headed up a flight of stairs, through a bare room with small windows overlooking the driveway, and on to the main clock tower.

"The clock is powered by large, suspended weights," Adrian told them, as they entered the small area where an enormous steel weight hung from a set of pulleys and descended slowly over the course of a number of days. "I wind the clock every Friday, and it's only Tuesday, so it isn't due to be wound again."

"How does it work?" Newman asked, peering at the old mechanics with boyish wonder.

"Well, to wind it up, you climb up this ladder to get to the top of the mechanism, through that wooden hatch," Adrian said, pointing towards a set of wooden ladders similar to those you might find in a loft. "When you go up, there's a ratchet which you lower on the left-hand side, to engage the cog. You fit this metal handle to the reduction gear, and wind up the larger of the two weights in an anticlockwise direction. Then, you fit the reduction gear and do the same with the spindle on the right-hand side, winding up the smaller weight in a clockwise direction. Gradually, the larger weight descends over the course of a few days, into that sort of pit, or well, over there."

Ryan turned away from his inspection of a brass dial, which told him the clock dated back to 1852, and moved across to a large, circular bed which had been built to accommodate the larger weight as the pendulum fell. As he approached it, he noticed that, although the weight had not yet reached its maximum depth, there appeared to be a blockage preventing it from descending further, thus causing the clock to stop.

Already knowing what he would find, Ryan leaned over the edge of the pendulum pit and, peering around the edge of the weight, saw the crumpled body of a man, his bones crushed beneath the relentless descent of an enormous steel ball.

"No need to wind up the clock," he said, in a flat, emotionless voice. "If you would please stop the mechanism, and then wait for me in the estate office?"

"My God, what's happened, now?" Newman exclaimed.

"Your head gardener is dead," Ryan told him. "And, since I'm fairly certain he wouldn't have bludgeoned his own skull before climbing into the bottom of this well so he could wait to be crushed by an enormous metal ball, I'll venture to say foul play is involved."

Adrian hurried to stop the mechanism from continuing to jam itself against Bullman's broken body, while Newman took himself off to find a stiff drink, and to have a word with his lawyers about the level of their insurance coverage.

CHAPTER 21

While Tom Faulkner captured photographs of Paul Bullman's body in situ before its removal to the mortuary, and Charlie Reed took care of interviewing the estate staff who would, no doubt, be uneasy at the prospect of a second murder having been committed at their place of work, Ryan and Phillips headed to one of the benches overlooking the ornamental gardens and sat down to think.

"At least I know one thing," Phillips said, popping a cashew nut into his mouth.

"I'm happy for you, Frank. We were all starting to wonder."

"Mind your cheek, and bend your ears," came the quick reply. "I was goin' to say, we know that Bullman was last seen around five o'clock last night. That means Bullman must've been dumped in that pit sometime in the evening, while there was still enough space to fit his body inside before the weight came down too far."

Ryan was in agreement. "Unless somebody was able to lift the weight—but I don't think so. It would have been enough effort to haul a body over the side as it is, never mind having to wind up the mechanism then wind it back down again. It invites too much uncertainty into an already risky situation."

"True, but then, some people don't mind taking risks—murderers, for example."

"You make a good point," Ryan said, with a short laugh. "But let's say your first theory is correct, and Bullman was put inside the pit before the weight reached him, that would indeed put the time of death somewhere between the hours of five and eight, depending on the rate of the mechanism's descent, and whether any of the other staff and residents can place Bullman alive after five o'clock."

"It would rule out a few of them," Phillips mused.

Ryan waited, watching a bird of prey rise up into the sky before swooping down again.

"For starters, all the daytime staff who usually work at Belsay weren't here, yesterday," Phillips continued. "The place was closed for our investigation, and it's still closed, so those staff haven't been needed on site."

Ryan nodded.

"As for those who live on the estate, we already know that a load of them have left, with our permission, to visit family over the Christmas period, so they would've been off-site during that time, n'all."

Ryan nodded again.

"Who does that leave?" Phillips asked, and then answered his own question. "Adrian and his wife, Sabrina, Quentin, Mark, Daisy and her mother and son, although I don't think her littleun would've had the strength."

Ryan had to agree. "Charlie's taking down their statements, now," he said. "Let's see whether any of them have an alibi."

He felt his mobile phone buzz to signal an incoming message, and retrieved it from his jacket pocket. "That's digital forensics," he said, after skim-reading a new e-mail. "They've managed to access Kimberley's phone records, which is a Christmas miracle, if ever I heard one. They've attached some text exchanges, just a moment—"

Ryan broke off to read the attachments, his expression growing darker by the minute.

"She was having an affair with Doctor Jones, as we suspected," he said, and tried not to feel repulsed by some of the content he was obliged to read. "Hold on…bloody hell, that's a surprise."

"For the love of God, you can't go around sayin' things like that without sharin' the gossip with your old pal," Frank said. "Now, howay, what's the juice then?"

Ryan slipped his phone back in his pocket.

"Frank, I need you to remain calm when I tell you the next piece of information, because I'm thinking of your blood pressure. Can you do that for me?"

"I can plant my boot up your arse, if that helps?"

Ryan grinned. "All right, then. It turns out, all three of the conservation team had been enjoying one another's company," he said, with a wiggle of his famous eyebrows. "There were some very spicy-looking exchanges between Kimberley and Quentin, but also between Kimberley and Sabrina."

Phillips' mouth formed an 'o' of surprise.

"Whey, I know it happens," he said, after a minute. "In fact, I used to know a lass who lived down the street from us, and she narf liked a bit of the old pampas grass—"

"I don't want to know," Ryan begged, of the universe in general.

"And I don't mind tellin' you, back when I was a youngun, there was a divorced lady who lived down in Whickham—gorgeous lookin', she was—and she happened to like a feller in uniform. Anyhow, she asked me whether I'd like to go along to one of her 'special parties'—"

"*Frank*," Ryan warned him. "I don't want to hear about your kinky sex games back in the seventies."

"Eighties!" Phillips exclaimed. "If there was any kinky sex happenin', it was happenin' in the eighties! I'm not that over the hill, y'nah!"

Charlie chose that precise moment to join them, and her delicate cough alerted both men to the fact she'd heard every word. "Is this a bad time?" she asked, while mirth danced in her eyes.

They jumped off the bench, as though it was made of hot coals.

"No, not at all—"

"Nope—"

"Good, because I was only going to update you with a summary of the witness statements," she said. "I can easily come back when Frank has finished telling you about the special parties he went to."

"It's alreet," Phillips said, waving that away. "It wasn't anythin' like that film, *Eyes Wide Shut,* if that's what you're thinkin'—"

"It wasn't what she was thinking," Ryan said, with absolute certainty, and Charlie laughed at the pair of them.

"Any idea who was the last person to see Bullman alive?" Phillips asked, having dragged himself back to business.

"Adrian, Mark and Daisy all say they saw Paul Bullman going into his farmhouse at around five or thereabouts," she said. "Adrian could see him from the window of his office, where he was closing things down for the evening, and Mark was on his way to the car park, so he happened to see him as he passed by."

"What was he doing in the car park?" Ryan wondered.

"Oh, he went out for dinner in Newcastle with some of the local landowners," she said. "He was gone until after midnight."

"Do we have that confirmed on the CCTV footage?" Ryan said.

"I can request it," she said.

"Assuming he hasn't told us any porky-pies, that puts Newman out of the picture during the relevant timescale," Ryan said. "What about the others?"

"Sabrina and Quentin say they were at his cottage, playing Scrabble all evening," Charlie said. "They both confirm the other's story."

"I'm sure they do," Ryan said. "We'll have a word with those two in a minute, because neither of them has been entirely honest with us about how well they knew Kimberley—" He broke off, as another e-mail buzzed in his pocket. "Sorry," he muttered, and paused to read another e-mail from the digital forensics team. "They've sent another batch of information, this time about her call data rather than texts. They'll cover social media apps and all that, next. As for calls…well, well. There was an outgoing call made to a phone registered to Mark Newman on the morning she died. I don't recall him mentioning having taken a call from Kimberley Foster, do you?"

They shook their heads.

"He might be alibied for Bullman's murder, but he could have driven up here in time to kill Kimberley Foster," Ryan said.

"Why, though?" Charlie wondered aloud. "What could he possibly stand to gain?"

"Perhaps it's not about gaining something, but rather about losing something," Ryan said, thoughtfully.

"We'll come to him, soon enough. First, let's have a word with the King of the Swingers."

They found Doctor Jones with Sabrina Fisher, deep in conversation over a collection of what appeared to be rare-looking coins laid out on the billiard table in the hall.

"May we have a word?" Ryan said.

"Again?" Sabrina said. "I've just given a statement to your constable, over there—"

"*Detective* constable, if you don't mind," Charlie corrected her, with a saccharine smile. "It seems some new evidence has come to light, which calls into question your version of events."

Quentin placed a hand over his heart, and tried to look shocked.

"*Sabrina*? Have you lied to the police? I would never have—"

"Save the act," Ryan snapped. "We're referring to both of you." He wandered over to look at the coins and his voice became dangerously quiet. "You told me and my team, on more than one occasion, that you only knew the late Kimberley Foster in a professional capacity. I'm going to ask you both again, what was your relationship with her?"

They looked at one another, and Quentin gave a negligent shrug of his linen-clad shoulders. "Fine, all right, I admit, I might have omitted certain elements—certain *private* elements of our relationship," he said. "I felt it was only right, given the poor girl had died. The last thing I want is for her family to think any the less of her."

"Why on Earth would they do that?" Phillips said.

"Look," Quentin said, with a touch of impatience. "Sabrina and I have been in a relationship for some time now, haven't we, sweetheart?"

He didn't wait for a reply.

"Occasionally, we invite new members of our team to join us in a little...recreational activity, you might say."

"Sex?" Ryan said bluntly, growing tired of the man's verbosity.

"Well, if you want to be crude about it...yes."

"So, you had a threesome going," Ryan said. "Then what?"

"Well, it was fine for a while, but it ran its course," Quentin said. "Things ended amicably between us and Kimberley, and we went back to a strictly professional relationship."

"When did this happen?"

"Oh—two, three weeks ago," Quentin said. "Water under the bridge."

"That's funny," Ryan said, turning to look at Frank and Charlie, then back at the two people shuffling nervously beside the billiards table. "We know that Kimberley had sexual intercourse on the day she died, at around lunchtime. Do you know of anyone else she might have been seeing?"

At this, Sabrina exploded, landing a hard hit on the side of Quentin's head. "You filthy liar!" she shouted. "You told me there was nothing going on behind my back, but you *lied*, didn't you? I *knew* it, when I couldn't find the pair of you, that lunchtime. I bloody *knew* it!"

She hit him again, for good measure, and the three police officers decided it was probably time to intervene.

"That's enough of that," Frank said, taking a firm grip on her arm.

Sabrina shrugged him off and turned to point at Quentin. "You want to know what really happened?" she said. "I'll tell you. We all had a few too many, one night, after raiding the cellars for some vintage wine. Quentin likes to help himself, while he's on a job, don't you, *darling*? Well, one thing led to another, and we spent the night together. As far as I was concerned, it was a one-off, drunken night, and that was all."

"It *was*," Quentin wailed. "You must believe me, sweetheart, you're the only girl—"

"Oh, shut up! Just shut up!" Sabrina shouted. "The next thing I knew, I was in an open relationship, and you were off being handcuffed to her bed every other night!"

"That explains the handcuffs," Frank whispered to Ryan, who gave him a look that told him clearly he was a buffoon.

"So, I guess you didn't like Kimberley very much, after all," Charlie said, slicing through the melodrama to try to find any motivation to kill.

"Well, of course not," Sabrina admitted. "Did you think we'd be best mates after that? But relationships are complicated, aren't they?"

Thankfully, it was a rhetorical question.

"Quentin's sorry, aren't you, darling?" No longer shouting and hitting, Sabrina was now stroking the side of Quentin's face, leaving them all dizzy with the sharp turnaround.

"Of course, I am," he crooned. "I made a mistake, that's all. I'm a weak man—I'd be nothing without you—"

"I think I'm gonna hurl," Charlie whispered to Frank.

"You and me both."

"You can save the make-ups for later," Ryan said, cuttingly. "I'd like fresh statements from the pair of you, and, in particular, I want to know whether Kimberley discussed anything that was on her mind, during your last assignation together."

Quentin looked sheepish, for Sabrina's sake, but they had the distinct impression he was enjoying the drama of it all. "It was the usual bedroom talk," he said, flipping back his fringe. "She said she might be leaving soon, but she'd let me know. To be honest, I was beginning to think that things were becoming too much of a juggle between the three of us, so I didn't object."

"Did she say why she was planning to leave?" Ryan pressed him.

"Something about a new opportunity," he said. "I'm sorry, I really can't remember."

"One final question, for now," Ryan said. "What was Kimberley working on, just before she died?"

"These coins, as far as I'm aware," Quentin said, gesturing to the collection, which must have been worth several thousand pounds to an avid collector. "They're Mediaeval, and the Trust—or, rather, I should say the new owner—wants to open a museum, here on site."

Ryan thought of another thing the digital forensics team had sent through to him, in their most recent e-mail. It was a record of some photographs taken by Kimberley of what looked like an old, leatherbound journal. He brought up the picture, and showed it to each of them, in turn.

"Do you recognise this book?" he asked.

Both Quentin and Sabrina shook their heads and, to his surprise, Ryan thought they might have been telling him the truth.

CHAPTER 22

While Frank and Charlie headed off to search Paul Bullman's farmhouse, Ryan went off to find the new baronet. In the end, he found Mark Newman sitting in his library in front of a roaring fire, reading one of the books he'd taken from a shelf, looking entirely at ease in his new surroundings.

"See?" Ryan said, from the doorway. "I told you, you'd get used to it."

"I have to confess, this place is growing on me," he admitted, and set the book down on a coffee table. "When I first came here, I was overwhelmed by the size of it, and the responsibility. Now…" He shrugged his broad shoulders. "I believe I can handle it," he said, with one of his easy smiles. "Is there anything I can help you with, Chief Inspector?"

"As a matter of fact, there is," Ryan said, and helped himself to one of the armchairs so that they were simply two gentlemen, discussing business.

At least, that was the impression he wanted to give.

"I'm told, by my digital forensics team, that you received a phone call from Kimberley Foster at eleven-oh-three on Sunday morning," he said, conversationally. "Is there any reason you didn't mention it?"

Newman seemed surprised by the news.

Then, he clicked his fingers.

"Ah, heck, I completely forgot," he said. "I *did* take a call from her on Sunday morning, but it only lasted a couple of minutes at the most, because I was about to go into a meeting, down in London."

That much could be true, Ryan thought, considering he'd already checked the location of Newman's phone when he'd taken the call. Sure enough, it had been in Central London.

That still left several hours for someone to drive north, in time to kill.

"What did Kimberley want to speak with you about?"

"Well, to be honest with you, mate, I was a bit surprised she even had my number," he replied. "I've never met the girl, after all. But I s'pose she must've gotten it from her boss, the doctor feller."

Ryan said nothing and Newman shrugged again. "She was on about havin' found somethin' important, in the walls of the strongroom," he said. "Now, between you and me, I haven't got the foggiest what a bloody *strongroom* is, when it's at home, but, any road, that's where she said she'd found somethin'."

"Did she tell you what it was?"

"No, like I said, I was on my way into a meeting," he said, staring off into the fireplace. "We only chatted for a minute or two. I s'pose I assumed she'd found jewellery, or somethin' like that? Although, why anyone would want to hide it in the walls of a strongroom, rather than in a safe, I don't know."

Ryan opened his mouth to enlighten him as to the purpose of a 'strong room', then thought better of it.

"Why do you think she was calling to tell you about it?" he asked instead. "Why go over her boss's head, for instance?"

Newman blew out his cheeks, and glanced at the fire again.

"Lord knows," he said. "She mustn't have trusted him, for one thing. Maybe she thought he'd try to steal it right from under me…or *maybe*, someone desperate for cash tried to steal it from *her*, and ended up killing her, instead?" Newman's eyes widened. "I bet I've only gone and cracked the case for you!"

"Any help is gratefully received," Ryan said, mildly, while he thought of the images Kimberley had taken of an old leather journal, including several of the inside pages.

What if there was something to lose, rather than something to gain?

His own words replayed in his mind, and it struck him that somebody who stood to lose a fortune could just as happily kill a young woman who was in the way, as somebody who stood to gain a fortune. In this case, Newman represented a little of both.

He needed to find that journal—

The truth struck him then, like an arrow between his eyes.

Ryan turned to look at the fire, which had simmered down to a steady glow now that it had finished burning through whatever had fed its flames just before he'd entered the room. Now, there was only a mountain of grey ash, where a stack of papers might once have been.

Or the inner pages of an old leather journal.

"Excuse me," Ryan said. "Enjoy the rest of your book. There was a time when people would burn them, you know."

Newman was silent for a long moment, then gave Ryan another of his bland smiles. "Who'd do such a thing?" he said, and tutted.

Ryan left and, as soon as he was out of sight, brought up the images Kimberley had stored on her phone and which had, mercifully, been backed up to her cloud storage facility, rendering her physical phone unnecessary. He fumbled with the attachments, cursing the slow download speed in that part of the world, and decided it would have been faster to run to Newcastle and back.

Eventually, the images reappeared, and he zoomed in on some of the old, looped handwriting, narrowing his eyes to read the cursive script on the small screen. He wasn't certain, but the pages she'd photographed seemed to read as follows—

1st December, 1890

Met Iris again, in the usual place. Still can't have enough of the honeyed nectar she offers, each time we touch, and there isn't another in the county to compare with her beauty. Gertie in the dark, as always, poor lamb. She really is a good sort, and so compliant. I know I must end things, soon; Iris is beginning to develop ideas above her station and will no longer accept presents or platitudes. She, a farmer's wife, fancies herself a lady.

And yet—

'Tis a pity she wasn't high born. She'd have dimmed the lights at any London gathering.

7th December, 1890

I grow tired of Iris. Her charms have always compelled me, enraged me, obsessed me. But now she goes too far. She demands I recognise the boy as my heir, which I can never do. Gertie carries my child, and that child will inherit. I will be lost without her, and sorry besides, but I must do what I must.

15th December, 1890

Tonight must be the very last time. I know I've said this, many times, and have been weak time and again. But, this evening, Iris told me she would go to Gertrude and tell her everything, then tell her husband about John's true parentage. She wishes to force my hand, though she says it's all for the boy.

He is a sweet-natured lad, and has his father's blonde good looks I daresay.

In other circumstances, he'd be a son to be proud of.

25th December, 1890

It happened, last night. I have ended it for all of us, and will never again succumb to such demands. She lies beneath the driveway, and Porter has closed up the entrances to the tunnel, which are a secret beyond the family circle and make it unlikely she will ever be found.

The lad was saddened, I am sure, but it can't be helped.

It is for the best.

The new constabulary descended upon the estate, their flat feet trampling the lawns while they scoured the place for clues. I watched them, from the library window, while Gertie played the piano.

In time, she will become a distant memory.

Ryan shut down the phone, and slipped it back inside his pocket, before reaching for it again. He called Anna, and waited while the number rang out. It was unusual for her not to take his calls, but then, perhaps she was working or lying down again, having felt unwell. He'd hoped to ask her to help him with a small matter of historical research, and then remembered there were two such boffins on site. He might not covet their private lives, but he assumed they knew how to compile a family tree.

He made directly for the billiard room.

CHAPTER 23

Frank and Charlie found a key to Bullman's farmhouse hidden beneath a threadbare doormat, and let themselves inside. The bones of the house were good, having been built during a time of solid craftmanship, and with stonemasonry to ensure heat retention in the winter and a cooler temperature in the summer. However, it had also been built in anticipation of housing a large, prosperous farmer's family with plenty of children and scullery maids to justify its size, rather than a single man of advancing years without any particular inclination towards cleaning or maintenance. Consequently, when they stepped inside the narrow stone hallway, they found it was a similar temperature to the air outside, which was hovering at around one or two degrees Celsius.

"It's Baltic in here," Frank said, and scrubbed his hands together to warm them up a bit. "You'd think he'd crank the heatin' up a bit!"

"He won't be doing anything, now," Charlie said, and turned into the first reception room, which was a living room. Much like the rest of the house, it was in a state of disrepair, with cracking plasterwork and wallpaper that looked as though it had been there since the coronation of Queen Victoria. Bare, badly scuffed floorboards were covered in a large, dirty wool rug, the original colour of which they couldn't have guessed. It was coated in all manner of crumbs and other detritus, but it was the thick bundles of dog hair that told them Paul Bullman hadn't lived alone, after all.

"Must have a hairy mutt," Frank remarked.

"There may be more than one," Charlie said, and cocked her ear to the sound of some plaintive *yaps*, coming from the back of the house.

There being nothing unusual to find in the living room, they followed the sound of dog barks and made their way towards an enormous kitchen. They imagined that, with a deep clean and possibly some fumigation, it would have been an impressive space, with the original wooden panelling and cabinetry still intact and contemporaneous with the house. At some point in the intervening years, someone had installed an ugly modern cooker, which stood at the end of a row of cabinets looking like the odd one out. The original fireplace looked as though it was often used to heat the room, and bore the charred remnants of several fires in its overflowing grate. A large table stood in the centre, covered in stains, scars, old newspapers and several dirty plates from meals gone by. From a door to the side, they heard insistent howling and the sound of claws scratching against woodwork.

"Are you okay with dogs?" Charlie asked, and Frank nodded.

"Aye, if they're friendly."

"Fingers crossed," she said, and grasped the door handle. "Ready to run?"

She didn't give him a chance to reply, but opened the door and, immediately, no fewer than six gigantic hounds burst into the room, barking and whining, circling and sniffing the most *intimate* of places.

"Here! Gerroff!" Phillips shooed away one of the dogs, only to be accosted by another.

"They must like your manly musk," Charlie said, with a chuckle.

"At least they're friendly," he agreed. "Bit *too* friendly, if y'ask me. Oi! Down! Good boy! *Here, man, I'm not a steak*!"

Frank proceeded to shuffle around the room in a kind of dance, as he tried to avoid the unwanted attentions of the small pack of over-friendly dogs.

"I wonder when they last ate," Charlie murmured, and made her way through to a large scullery and boot room area, which was now the dogs' domain—and smelled like it, too.

"Or when they last used the netty," Frank pointed out. "Howay, lads, I'll take you outside for a *walk*—"

Instantly, the dogs began to bark with excitement.

"You said the wrong word," Charlie laughed. "Maybe they'll be happy with a quick run around the garden? In the meantime, I'll try to find some food around here, and top up their water bowls."

Frank muscled his way through the 'lads' and battled a rusted lock on the back door until it finally budged.

"Well, stand back!" he told them and, remarkably, they seemed to understand.

The instant the fresh air hit their noses, they bounded off into the overgrown lawn and raced around like a set of teenage boys up to no good.

"This grass has seen better days," Frank said to himself, eyeing the old mounds of dog excrement littering the turf. "But at least it's fertile…"

He let them fertilize it a bit more, before calling them back inside.

"Alreet! Howay back inside!"

When that didn't work, he tried another universal message.

"GRUB'S UP!"

Something in his tone had probably been the deciding factor but, for all the world, he'd have sworn they spoke the same language. Instantly, the dogs turned, ears pricked, and then raced back towards the house. Seeing their solid, muscular bodies paired with jaws that could crack bones, Frank almost turned and fled in the other direction. However, something in their eyes told him there was no threat, and so he remained where he was, ready to administer a scratch around the ears to whichever dog fancied one.

One of the hounds gave him such a look of adoration, he was moved.

"Now, then, that's enough of all that," he said, with mock severity. "I've got plenty on me plate without havin' to think about walkin' a dog, feedin' a dog, and all that malarkey."

The dog continued to look at him with big, puppy-dog eyes.

"Maybe it'd be good to have another man around the house," Frank thought aloud. "The lasses have got me outnumbered, so I need all the help I can get."

He continued to ruffle the dog's ears.

"Ryan's got a dog," he continued, as if they were a couple of old pals. "If he can manage a dog, I'm sure I can manage a dog—"

Just then, Charlie called out to let them know the kibble was ready and waiting.

"Go on, lad, and get your dinner," he said. "You'll be clammin', by now. I know I am."

The dog gave his hand a final, parting lick, and then loped back inside.

"Find anything?"

Having left the dogs to hoover up their food, Frank and Charlie resumed their search of the farmhouse.

They worked room-by-room, looking with gloved hands for signs of anything that might give them a clue about why Paul Bullman had been killed.

"Well, at least there's no handcuffs, this time," Frank mumbled, as he closed the drawer of a rickety bedside table.

"What's that?" Charlie said, from her position crouched on the floor, where she was peering under the bed.

"Never mind! Looks like Paul had a touch o' diabetes," he said, noting a stack of medication sitting atop an equally rickety chest of drawers. "I can't understand what Kimberley Foster and Paul Bullman have in common, here. Why did someone need both of them dead?"

Charlie stood up again, brushing the hair and fluff from her jeans. "Kim took those pictures—the ones of the old leather journal, remember? I haven't had a chance to look at them closely, but maybe there was something in those pages? There had to be something, otherwise I can't imagine what possible reason anyone would have for killing her."

"Aye, Sabrina seems the jealous type, and she's not averse to administering a clip round the ears," Frank thought aloud. "But I wouldn't peg her as bein' jealous enough, or daft enough, to kill for that auld duffer she's shacked up with."

"Love does funny things," Charlie averred, and began searching the man's wardrobe to keep her hands busy. "She could have met Kimberley up there, intending to have a private word warning her to stay away from her man, and all that. Who knows? Maybe Kim was completely smitten with the dapper Doctor Jones, and didn't want to back away without a fight…so, Sabrina gave her a shove, but didn't know her own strength. She panicked, wiped away her fingerprints on the door leading out to the roof, and hurried back to her cottage before anybody could find her—but not before slipping into the neighbouring cottage and stealing Kim's mobile phone." Charlie paused. "Although, how would she gain entry?"

Frank opened his mouth, but then she waved a hand.

"*Maybe* it wasn't about love, at all," Charlie continued, excitedly. "What if Sabrina's in it for the money, and that's why she and Mr Lover-Lover make such a good match? Let's say Kim found that old journal, and whatever was written inside it was important enough to impact Sabrina and Quentin's pocket, in some way or another. It could have given the directions to an enormous Mediaeval haul of gold, for all we know. Now, if Sabrina and Quentin have it in mind to find that pot of gold and keep it for themselves, maybe sell it on the black market, perhaps Kim decided to extort them for a bit of ready cash—by threatening to tell the new owner all about their sticky fingers with the family heirlooms, or something like that?"

"That's not a bad theory," Frank said, listening avidly. "Go on, what happened next?"

"Well, Kim might've hidden the journal and told them she wouldn't hand it over until they gave her a big fat wad of cash," Charlie said, painting a vivid picture of the machinations that could have occurred. "They decide to meet on the roof, two of them or even all three of them and, by hook or by crook, they manage to get hold of her mobile phone before shoving her through the glass. They think that by taking the mobile phone they'll be safe from the prying eyes of the police, but they didn't reckon for our crack team of hotshots being in the building that night."

Frank laughed. "You had me goin' there," he said. "In fact, I wouldn't be surprised if there's a kernel of truth somewhere in all that. But the bottom line is, we don't have any evidence to say whether any of it happened. It could just as easily have been Adrian or one of the others who did for Kim Foster, for similar reasons. How about Bullman, though? Where does he come into it?"

"He might've wanted a bit of the action, but nobody wanted to share," Charlie suggested. "He might've seen one of them fleeing the scene…could've tried blackmailing the killer and ended up getting more than he bargained for."

Frank thought of the shabby furnishings in the cold house without adequate heating, and the bargain basement food they'd found in its bare cupboards.

"This place definitely gives the impression he was hard up for money," Frank said. "Blackmail might've been a temptation for him, rather than comin' straight to the police, that's for sure."

"Which still begs the question—why? What had Kimberley found?"

"I have a few ideas about that," Ryan said.

Both Frank and Charlie almost jumped out of their respective skins.

CHAPTER 24

"HOLY MOLY!" Phillips cried, flattening himself back against the nearest wall. "Why do you have to sneak around the place, like that?"

"Can I help it, if I tread lightly?" Ryan asked.

"There's treadin' lightly, then there's movin' like the undead," Frank argued. "You might as well be bleedin' Dracula, the way you hover about."

Ryan made a show of licking his lips, in the manner of Leslie Nielsen in Mel Brooks' classic, slapstick comedy, *Dracula: Dead and Loving It*.

"You said you had some ideas," Charlie prompted, after Ryan and Frank had finished lambasting one another. "What did Kimberley find that was so important?"

"Look at what's written on the pages," he said, calling up the images to his phone once more. "They're old diary entries, from December 1890. I've done a bit of quick online research, and even had a word with our resident swingers, to try to get a historic perspective. The diary seems to have belonged to William Edgington, who was the eighth baronet, here at Belsay. The 'Gertie' he refers to must be his wife, Gertrude. Her son, also called William, became the ninth baronet, when his father died prematurely in 1895, at the age of thirty-three."

The other two made sympathetic noises, though they'd never met Gertrude Edgington, nor any of her descendants.

"How did her husband die?" Frank found himself wondering.

"He seems to have died in an accidental shooting incident on his own estate, here," Ryan said. "I couldn't find much about it, except a local gazette piece which said that the man responsible was a former resident of this very farmhouse—a tenant farmer called Frederick Webster. More interesting still is the fact that the newly-formed Northumberland County Police Constabulary decided not to prosecute him for the death, which is an unusual move, considering Edgington was an aristocrat and Webster a lowly farmer, by relative standards at the time."

Charlie had been reading the extracts while Ryan talked, but now she looked up and passed them to Frank.

"These diary extracts seem to suggest Edgington had a mistress called Iris," she said. "And an illegitimate son, if I'm reading them correctly? It seems he ended the relationship—"

"I think he may have done much more than that," Ryan said. "I think that last diary entry is a confession, of sorts.

I think William Edgington killed his mistress, and got away with it."

"But who was Iris?" Charlie wondered aloud. "There must be some way of finding out who she was."

"I know who she was."

They waited.

"The suspense is killin' us," Frank whispered, to break the tension.

Ryan grinned. "Let's see…for a start, there's no record anywhere of William Edgington having fathered an illegitimate child. I don't think any of his contemporaries would have been surprised by that, necessarily, given the man's reputation as a gambler and womaniser, but nothing was ever 'on the record' and Edgington never admitted or legitimised anyone, legally, as far as the records show."

"How does that help us?"

"Have patience, young padawan," Frank told her. "He's workin' up to it. Mind you, he could hurry up, a bit, since I'm not gettin' any younger."

"Point taken," Ryan said, and tried to abridge things, for an impatient audience. "I was interested in the farmer who shot his master, supposedly by accident, and so I did a bit of digging. It turns out poor Frederick Webster had been married a few years earlier to a great beauty, who vanished overnight on Christmas Eve in 1890."

"He killed her, you mean?" Frank said.

Ryan shook his head. "He was investigated, but there was no evidence to suggest Fred Webster was anything other than a devoted husband, and a devoted father to his five-year-old son," he said. "Do you want to guess what his wife was called?"

The other two smiled, as the jigsaw pieces began to come together.

"Iris," Charlie said. "Now, that's quite a coincidence."

"And we all know how you feel about those," Frank interjected, before Ryan could tell them again. "You reckon this Iris was Edgington's mistress, the one he's talkin' about in his diary, here?"

"The one he seems to be saying he killed, because she was asking too much of him, and demanding legitimacy for their son," Ryan said. "Yes, I think it's one and the same."

"How many children did Webster have?" Charlie asked, following the trail of breadcrumbs with ease.

"Just the one," Ryan said, and nodded to the unspoken question. "Yes, I think the boy—John Webster—was William Edgington's biological child, though John probably never knew it."

"Do you suppose Fred Webster found out about the affair, or suspected that Edgington had killed his wife or sent her away?" Charlie asked.

"I think Iris never left these grounds," Ryan said, with another enigmatic smile.

"Bloody hell, there he goes again," Frank muttered, and had a sudden, overwhelming urge to eat something sugary. "You're gettin' as bad as Pinter."

"Well, it is panto season," Ryan said, defensively. "I'm allowed a bit of showmanship, every now and again—"

"Oh, no you're not," Charlie said, quick as a flash.

Phillips laughed in his inimitable way, and gave her a nudge.

"That was a goodun," he chuckled.

"One tries," she said, loftily.

"Look, do you want to know where Iris Webster is buried or not?"

"He says something about her being under the driveway," Charlie said. "Does he mean he managed to kill and hide her body before the groundworks were laid?"

"It's far simpler than that," Ryan said. "There's a tunnel that runs beneath part of the driveway, just past the courtyard in front of the stables and the old kitchens. It ends a bit further along, closer to the front of the hall. When I spoke to Quentin and Sabrina, they were more than accommodating, especially when I mentioned that theft was most definitely a criminal offence, as was fraud—oh, and I threw indecent exposure into the mix, as well."

"They've not had it off on the bloody roof, have they?" Frank said, in horrified, if mildly envious tones.

"Not that I'm aware of, but, as you so eloquently put it, they look the *type*."

Frank nodded.

"The point is, they were only too keen to show me what they'd found amongst some of the old house plans and other old paperwork," Ryan continued. "One very old plan showed that underground tunnel, which seemed not to have been widely known about beyond the family. According to household records, both entrances at either end of the tunnel were sealed off and access was strictly denied from then on."

"When did this happen?" Charlie asked, but might have guessed the answer.

"Late December, 1890—not long after Iris Webster's disappearance."

There was a long pause, as each of them considered the widespread ramifications of this new information.

"If you're right, and Edgington not only murdered his mistress, but hid her body in a tunnel which has been blocked off for more than a hundred and thirty years, why would this be so contentious?" Charlie asked. "I know it's a case of murder, which is interesting, but why did this information move somebody to murder Kim?"

Ryan's eyes shone, because he knew the answer to everything was so close.

So close, now, he could almost touch it.

CHAPTER 25

Ryan heard the rumble of a police van and several squad cars crunching across the gravel driveway somewhere outside, and he paused in his storytelling to move to one of Bullman's bedroom windows, which faced the hall. Sure enough, he spotted several unmarked cars arriving without any sirens, which was in keeping with the instructions he'd given them half an hour ago. Soon, he knew, the police and forensics staff would spill out of their vehicles and begin setting up another cordon around the courtyard access to the underground tunnel, where they would go about the business of finding out whether Iris Webster was the hall's resident ghost, after all.

Content to be avenging the dead, he turned his mind back to the living.

"Iris may have died, but John Webster, her son with William Edgington, lived on," Ryan said, picking up the story. "He married, and had children, some of whom had children themselves. That's all I know, without the help of an expert genealogist, so I've called one to come and do the heavy lifting for us. Hopefully, they can tell us about who might be one of John's direct descendants and whether they're still alive."

"Why does it matter, since there's already an heir to Belsay," Charlie asked, not quite grasping the point as quickly as she usually would, since she'd suffered a late night with a restless toddler.

"It matters because Newman is descended from a very distant line, rather than being directly descended from William Edgington. He's the great-great-great nephew of one of Edgington's second cousins, because that's the closest they could find in probate," Ryan said. "Whereas, if somebody could prove they were from a closer line of descendants, even illegitimately, they would have the prior claim to the house, estate, money, title… everything."

"The kind of fortune some folk'd kill for," Frank surmised.

"Exactly," Ryan said. "Kim found the diary, and put two and two together. She wanted to get away and move on to better things, but she needed money. Lo and behold, she stumbled across the diary while she was exploring the house and its passageways, including one that took her through to the strong room, where all the household valuables used to be kept."

"I suppose she already knew a bit about the family tree, and the sort of man Edgington seems to have been,"

Charlie said. "She knew that a word in the ear of the right person might set her up for a very long time to come."

Ryan nodded.

"She also knew her mark wouldn't want to hand everything over, when he'd only just acquired it, and was looking forward to a very different standard of living to the one he'd been accustomed to."

"*Newman*?" Frank said.

Ryan nodded. "Who else?"

"But—how? How would he know about any of the this?"

"He's been kept up to date with the conservation team's progress, so he'd have known a bit about his family background," Ryan said. "Then, last Sunday morning, Kimberley called him. She got the number from Quentin's phone, probably while he was sleeping it off—"

"Eww," Charlie said, and Ryan made an apologetic face.

"Sorry, try not to think about it," he said. "Anyway, my best guess is that she called him to talk about the journal, and what it was worth to him if she chose to hand it over and keep quiet. She probably had to spell everything out for him, since I don't think I'm incorrect in saying, our new baronet isn't exactly the hottest burger on the barbie, as it were."

Frank snorted.

"Unfortunately, Kim didn't really know anything about the estate's new owner, so she underestimated the danger. Thanks to a very illuminating search of the international database, I happen to know Mr Newman was adept at all manner of petty and some more serious crimes, and has an extensive record. Our friends in Melbourne were glad to be rid of him, I'm sure."

"So, rather than paying out any of his new money, he killed her," Charlie said, trying to imagine the kind of greed that would be so strong as to take precedence over the sanctity of life. "But he wasn't in the North East when Kim died, and he was in Newcastle when Bullman died, so how could he have committed either murder?"

"Newman only *told* us he stopped off in Yorkshire," Frank put in. "He could've driven straight up from London."

"I've put in a request for ANPR footage from the North Circular and the A1 northbound out of London," Ryan added. "That'll take a few days…probably longer, since people will be clocking off work in time for Christmas. Still, it'll give us some answers."

"I don't understand how Newman would he know where to meet Kimberley, or how to get into the house using the side door," Charlie said.

"I think Kimberley chose the meeting place, to her great misfortune," Ryan said. "The upper floor was probably somewhere she thought nobody would look, so their meeting wouldn't be disturbed. She knew it couldn't be accessed easily from the main part of the house, where our event was taking place, and her other colleagues had clocked off for the week. Kim couldn't have known that she was dealing with a vicious opportunist, who would have seen the possibilities in a readymade set-up like that. I think she left the door open for him, and even gave him directions over the phone."

Ryan moved to look out of the window at the parkland beyond, thinking of a young woman with so much life left to live. Kimberley Foster was of a similar age to his sister, when she'd been murdered, and he thought for the umpteenth time that there was a fundamental truth to the work they did. That is, the majority of the most brutal acts were committed by men upon other men. However, when it came to subtle, sexually-aggravated or control-based attacks, they were usually perpetrated by men towards women, because a physical disparity made them vulnerable to a certain kind of person. As a father, a husband, a son and a friend to women, he had often wished things were different, and that a certain class of men in the world didn't choose to thank their women for loving them, caring for them and bearing their children by hitting, punching, biting, bludgeoning, raping and killing them.

But it was a cycle.

It was all a cycle that needed to be broken, and he and his team did their part.

"I had a look at Kim's call record again," he said. "Two minutes is a surprisingly long time to talk, don't you think? It's certainly long enough for Kim to set out her demands and give him some instructions about where to meet. She probably thought she was safe, with so many police officers nearby, which has a certain irony to it."

Ryan's jaw tightened.

She should have been safe, he thought.

"Newman's either fearless, arrogant, or both, just as we suspected when this first happened," he said, turning back to his friends. "He wasn't concerned in the slightest about killing her, nor about getting away with it."

"Where does Bullman come into all this?" Frank wondered aloud. "Did he know about the journal too?"

Ryan gave a slight shake of his head. "I doubt it," he replied. "No, I think Bullman was another kind of opportunist. He actually *told* us what he'd seen, that first time we met him. Do you remember?"

The other two looked at him as though he'd sprouted three heads, and Ryan muttered something rude.

"Bullman talked quite a lot about the possibility of someone having hiked across the fields, after parking in one of the lay-bys on the edge of the estate, before contradicting himself completely by saying it was very unlikely," he reminded them. "At the time, I didn't think much of it, except that he was doing a bit of amateur sleuthing. Only now do I think he was saying it for Newman's benefit—he was standing beside us, listening, the whole time."

"You think he was alerting him to the fact he'd been seen?" Charlie said. "Why then? Why not speak to him in private?"

"I think Bullman might have wanted to show Newman that he meant business," Ryan said. "By saying all that in the presence of the senior investigating officer assigned to the case, he's clearly not messing about. He probably hoped it would have encouraged Newman to cough up the money without delay."

"Just like Kim, he didn't really understand who—or *what*—he was dealing with," Charlie said, with a degree of sympathy. "He bought the whole 'Nice Aussie' act; hook, line and sinker. Newman would *never* have paid him, and he has so little impulse control and such an appetite for risk, he probably enjoyed the thrill of having it spoken about in front of the police."

"Probably made him feel superior," Frank chipped in. "These buggers love to feel like they're clever."

"Whereas Mr Newman isn't clever, at all," Ryan said, with brutal honesty. "He's sloppy, impulsive, as you say, and driven by greed. It makes people prone to errors, such as stealing a mobile phone from a dead woman, or wiping fingerprints off a well-used door handle."

"How did he manage to kill Bullman?" Frank said. "He was definitely at that dinner, in town."

"Ah, yes." Ryan smiled. "I had a look at the CCTV from the parking area, then compared it with the only other working camera, which is by the main gates. I timed it myself, to see how long it would take the average driver to cover the distance from the car park to the main gates, and it's approximately four minutes—"

"Make that six, since you're not the 'average' driver," Frank said.

"Fine, let's make it an even five," Ryan said. "Anyway, the time lapse between the two cameras capturing Newman leaving the car park and hitting the main gates on his way out was twelve minutes. That's a difference of seven minutes which can't be accounted for—unless..."

He moved back to the window, and pointed to the clock tower, which was visible from where they stood.

"There's a slot between the trees, over there, where he could have parked up for a few minutes, under cover of darkness," Ryan said. "People are mostly keeping indoors, since it's so cold, so the chance of being caught was slim, especially as the usual staff aren't around to come and go. It would've been easy to jump out and head into the clock tower to conduct a planned exchange, where he'd be met by Bullman. Faulkner can confirm it for us, but I think he cracked the man's skull against the side of the wall, to disable him, and then strangled him or asphyxiated him in some other way—his face looked very bloated, when I first discovered the body."

"What about getting Bullman into the pit?" Charlie said. "It's no easy task to lift a man like that."

"Have you seen the bloke?" Frank said. "Newman's been eatin' his greens all his life, by the looks of it. He's packin' a load of muscle and he's tall. It might've taken a bit of effort, but he could've done it."

They fell silent, imagining the grunts and groans of a man struggling to offload a dead weight.

"What now?" Frank asked, after a long pause.

Ryan broke into a smile. "I'd have thought you'd know this, by now, but, when we have a suspect, we perform something called an *arrest*—"

"Better watch your step, lad, or else you'll have somethin' to arrest *me* for."

On which ominous note, they went in search of a pair of handcuffs.

CHAPTER 26

As they were leaving the farmhouse, Mark Newman stepped out of the estate office and into the courtyard to find the place swarming with police personnel.

"What's goin' on here?" he demanded. "Have you found somethin'?"

"If you wouldn't mind stepping away from the police line, sir, we would appreciate it," one of the sentry officers told him, in the polite, detached tone of one who was used to dealing with difficult people.

"Hey, this is my place!" he almost shouted. "I've got a right to know what the bloody hell's goin' on!"

"*Sir,*" she said. "I'm going to ask you once again. *Please move away.*"

"Everything okay here?" Ryan enquired, with one of his brightest smiles, which he reserved for those he loved and, occasionally, those he loathed.

"Not really, mate," Newman said. "What's the idea havin' all of these uniforms settin' up shop in the middle of the driveway?"

"Ah, well, in the first place, they're all here to find a body that we believe to be hidden in a tunnel beneath the driveway here," Ryan said, conversationally. "It's accessed through an old storm drain, which was covered over and blocked up a long time ago. We're opening it up again."

"Who gave you permission—"

"I don't need permission," Ryan said, and his voice cracked like a whip. "In the second place, Mr Newman, I'm not your mate. I am, however, your worst nightmare at this very moment, because I'm afraid the fun's over. Mark Newman, I am arresting you for the murders of Kimberley Foster and Paul Bullman—"

"You've gotta be kidding!"

They saw the mask slip away from him. The affable, slightly dozy, tanned surfer from Australia with his small-town charm and inexperience gave way to the sly swindler and violent killer that lay beneath the blond hair and waxed jacket.

"—you have the right to remain silent, but anything you do say—"

It happened very suddenly, then.

One moment, Newman was standing there, the next, he'd taken off at a sprint. In a matter of seconds, he'd evaded four police constables, all of whom tried but failed to grab him as he fled.

"For f—sake," Ryan muttered, and then took off at full pelt after him.

Charlie followed closely behind, her legs pumping hard and fast to keep pace with the two men who had a head start on her.

Phillips watched them for a few moments, then shook his head at the folly of youth. "Oi! C'mere a minute!" he called over to the nearest constable.

"Sir?"

"Listen, go inside and fetch one of Newman's socks, or something else he's worn recently—a coat, hat, anything, so long as it smells of him. Alreet?"

The constable looked bemused, but hurried off to obey the direction, returning less than two minutes later bearing a woollen sweater. "The—the manager in there says this belongs to Mr Newman—"

"Good work, lad. Now, the next thing is…are you afraid of dogs?"

The constable shook his head, even more bemused than before. "Dogs, sir?"

"Aye, lad. That's what I said. Mind, keep an eye on your balls, because they're not shy."

Ryan's legs covered the ground at speed, but his muscles felt the burn as he swooped and swerved through the foliage surrounding the main hall, all the while keeping his eye on the retreating figure running as though Satan himself was in pursuit. They were heading in the direction of the quarry garden, Ryan knew, and it wasn't long before they passed beneath an enormous set of craggy stone pillars, almost curved to an arch, beyond which was a kind of Eden.

The light was already starting to fade, casting long shadows along a densely verdant pathway, which wound like a jagged fault line through the quarried rock. What might once have been stark, now bloomed with life, rare flowers and plants from remote corners of the world having taken up residence in their new home to lend colour and vibrancy to the broken stone.

Ryan saw all this as he gave chase, and thought that he'd like to come back and walk the route again in happier circumstances, with Emma on his shoulders, as she usually was during their outings. Now, there was no time to enjoy the gentle buzz of bees and other insects in the undergrowth, or to wonder at frost clinging to the delicate strands of a cobweb. There was only the sound of his own racing heartbeat, the thunder of his feet against the pathway, and Charlie's, a short distance behind him. He thought he heard a dog barking, somewhere, and then—

Then, he heard them.

Ryan turned to look over his shoulder, slowing down briefly to make sense of the new noise, and suddenly they appeared. Six enormous hounds emerged on the pathway, advancing swiftly with their noses in the air, their impressive hind legs propelling them forth with single-minded intent. Though he'd grown up around all kinds of farm animals, Ryan experienced a flutter of fear; the same fear he imagined a fox might feel in the wild, with these born hunters coming for it without prejudice or mercy.

"Charlie—look out!"

He watched her jump aside to avoid being swept off her feet, and he was forced to do the same, rearing back to the edge of the pathway to allow the dogs to continue onward, their howls signalling that they'd scented their quarry and wouldn't stop until they'd found him.

Having also heard the coming onslaught of a pack of rampaging dogs, Mark Newman found himself a high stone ledge upon which to perch until the coast was clear. Unfortunately for him, the dogs had been well-trained not to kill, but to bark loudly and incessantly until a person of authority came to apprehend the fox—or, in this case, a grown man balancing precariously on a ledge.

When Ryan and Charlie reached him, Newman was trying, foolishly, to scale the wall, his impractical shoes sliding against the slippery rock, the skin of his fingertips rubbed raw and bleeding as he tried to drag himself higher.

"I don't think that's a very good idea, do you?" Ryan called up. "Why don't you come back down, and we'll have a nice little chat at police headquarters?"

"Bugger off!" Newman called back.

"Fair enough!" Ryan said. "But, just to let you know, I'm going to leave the dogs here. They look a bit hungry, but I'm sure they can wait until dinnertime."

"This is—police brutality!"

"Is it? Well, I'm sure you know all about brutality, don't you, Mark?"

"I dunno what you're goin' on about!"

"Oh, I think you do! We can stay here, all night, if you want, but I'd much rather conduct an interview in a relatively warm but uninspiring interview room, rather than out here, in the cold."

"This is a disgrace!" Newman shouted, and, this time, they noted a touch of desperation in his voice.

Good, Ryan thought, wickedly.

"I've got rights!"

"So did Kimberley, and so did Paul!"

"I'm—I'm important!" Newman tried again, even more desperately than before.

"I've heard it all, now," Ryan muttered, and Charlie smiled.

"I'm a baronet, for God's sake! That has to mean somethin'!"

"Well, if it does, then I'm sorry to tell you that you won't be a baronet for very long," Ryan said.

Newman fell silent.

"You know what I'm talking about, don't you, Mark? You know there's somebody out there who, simply by being alive, can take all of this newfound wealth and privilege away from you. It must have been pretty hard, finding that out, eh?"

Newman continued to say nothing, but rested his forehead against the rock. Meanwhile, several feet below him, one of the dogs took a strong liking to Charlie and made his intentions clear.

"*Hey*!" she squealed, and pushed his impertinent snout away. "I'm not your type!"

Ryan held back a smile, and focused on getting their prime suspect back onto solid ground. "Mark, it's almost Christmas, and we all want to go home," he said. "The last thing any of us want to be doing is standing out here in the freezing cold, waiting for you to lose your grip and fall. Then, I'll have to call an ambulance, and that means more paperwork. I'll have to file an accident report, and all sorts of bureaucratic crap that'll put me in a stinking bad mood when I come to interview you under caution. So, what do you say? Shall we move this conversation inside?"

Newman seemed to consider things, and then nodded.

As he came down, Charlie held back the dogs through sheer force of pheromones, but was prepared for the man to do something stupid, again.

This time, he tried to land a punch on Ryan's jaw, which was dodged easily.

"Assaulting a police officer, now? You just keep racking up the charge sheet, don't you?"

With that, he planted a boot behind the man's knees and brought him to the ground in one smooth motion.

CHAPTER 27

Ryan and Charlie deposited Mark Newman into a squad car, corralled the dogs into some kind of order until it could be decided what to do with them, and then went in search of the Dog Whisperer himself.

They found Phillips deep in conversation with a young boy dressed in school uniform, who introduced himself as Henry Flowers-Mayhew. He was tall for his age, with pale blond hair and eyes the colour of the Mediterranean sea. They imagined he would be a menace to the girls, thereabouts, in a few years' time; for the present, he was a well-mannered, shy little boy whose mother had given permission for him to speak to the friendly sergeant and quiz him all about what it was like being a policeman.

"Do robbers really wear stripy tops?" he was asking, when Ryan and Charlie moved forward to join the conversation. "And do they carry sacks?"

Phillips' eyes twinkled. "Well, to be honest with you, son, they usually wear grubby old joggers and a hoodie, in my experience," he replied. "But, then again, I've never met a fancy jewel thief, or someone who goes around stealin' yachts—"

"What about planes?"

"Aye, there's folk that hijack planes," he replied.

"What did he do?" the boy asked, pointing towards the car where Mark Newman was currently being held before transfer to the station.

"We think he might have hurt some people," Frank said, carefully. "So we're goin' to ask him a few questions about it."

The boy nodded. "Are you the boss?" he asked Ryan, tipping his head up to look at the tall man with the black hair and kind eyes.

"I try to be," he replied. "Unfortunately, I have a lot of wayward staff, who go about releasing hound dogs without permission, and things like that."

"That's what you call 'showing initiative', and I hope you're makin' a note of it, for my next performance review," Frank said. "It's lateral thinkin' that saves the day, not bein' a fast runner."

Ryan had to admit, he'd questioned his own sense in giving chase to a man several years his junior, who was in peak physical fitness. He kept in shape himself, and was athletic without being an athlete. That meant he could mostly keep up with pursuing anyone on foot, but he felt it a lot more now than he ever did.

Age, he thought, irritably.

He spent most of his life looking forward, not back; and yet, newfound limitations such as a reduced running speed forced him to address his own mortality. Would there come a time when he could no longer run after a suspect, and instead must employ some of Phillips' lateral thinking strategies, instead? Of course, there would. The time was almost nigh, he thought with even more irritation.

It might be coming, Ryan thought. *But it wasn't there, yet.*

Just then, Tom Faulkner emerged from the storm drain on the other side of the driveway, and put his thumb up.

"What does he mean?" Henry asked. "Is he asking if you're okay?"

"No, lad," Frank said, softly. "He's lettin' us know they've found somethin'."

"What?"

"I'll tell you another time, young man," Frank said, keeping up a cheerful demeanour for the boy's benefit. "Now, run along and see your ma, she'll have your dinner on the table, I'm sure."

Henry scrambled off the bench where they'd been sitting, thanked Frank for telling him all about the police, and then ran as fast as his legs could carry him to where his mother, Daisy, waited for him beside the cordon.

"He's dropped something," Ryan said, and bent down to pick up a heavy gold pocket watch, with a faded inscription that listed the names of its previous owners, all of whom were former baronets. "I don't think this is his, after all. It must belong to Newman."

Frank shook his head, considering. "No, it can't belong to him," he said. "All its past owners were the bleedin' head honcho of everythin'. Even a curious young lad would know that was out of bounds to pilfer, if he had the chance."

Ryan wasn't so sure. "We should ask him where he got it," he replied. "There might be some explanation. *Henry!*" he called out, and the boy ran back. "Do you mind telling me where you got this?"

"It was my mummy's," Henry replied. "She used to travel a lot, so she gave it to me."

"This watch belonged to your mum?" Ryan said, and compelled the boy to focus. "Tell me, Henry—do you know where she got it?"

He shook his head.

"She didn't get it from a shop, or anything like that," he said. "She got it from my grandma, who got it from her dad, when he died."

"And, he was?"

"Gerald Webster was my great-grandad," he replied, having recently learned how to decipher family trees. "He was a farmer here and he had my grandma, Catherine, who married my grandad Pete, who was a gardener here, and they had my mum, Daisy."

"I see," Ryan said, and the three police officers looked at one another in what could only be described as sheer excitement. "Do you mind if we come and have a word with your mum, Henry?"

He shook his head, and led them over to where she awaited him, chatting to Adrian about the drama that had unfolded in the past hour.

"Chief Inspector," she said, holding out a hand to her son and nodding to the others. "Thank you for letting him come and talk to some 'real life police officers'. He was so excited when he saw some of the uniformed officers arrive."

Henry nodded, and leaned against his mother's leg.

"Is it true, what we've heard about Mark Newman?"

"We've arrested him, yes," Ryan said, without using unpleasant words like 'murder' which could offend small ears.

"Well, I can hardly believe it," she said, and sounded very genuine. "Why did he do it?"

"We have some theories about that," Ryan said, glanced down at Henry with a smile, and then turned to Adrian. "I wonder, could we borrow your office for a few minutes?"

The estate manager spread his arms. "Of course, help yourself."

Daisy looked between Ryan and Phillips, and then out of the window towards her son, who was playing a game of football with Adrian, on the lawn outside. Charlie had left to collect her own little boy, and Daisy remembered those early years with Henry, after his father died, and how hard the juggle could be, at times.

"I—I don't think I understand," she said, and swallowed to relieve a dry throat. "You're saying you think one of my ancestors, Iris Webster, has been found in a tunnel beneath the driveway?"

Ryan nodded. "We believe she was murdered by another of your ancestors, William Edgington."

She shook her head. "He's no relation of mine," she said, feeling happy to be able to correct their mistake. "My family have always worked on the estate here, but there's never been any married ties with the family in the main house—"

"Let me explain the connection, Ms Flowers," Ryan said, and proceeded to set out the familial story as he'd told it to Charlie and Frank.

By the end, Daisy looked pale. "I can't take this in," she whispered. "You—you believe that we—that my son, Henry, is the true heir to this estate?"

"It isn't a question of belief, so much as a question of DNA," Ryan said. "If you'll consent to a sample being taken, we can find out pretty quickly whether what we think is true, is actually the case."

Daisy nodded, and was silent for a long, long moment. "And, if he is, what then?"

They didn't know how to answer.

"We don't have much, detectives, but we're happy," she explained. "I don't want my son to change for the worse, or become entitled because of inherited wealth. I don't want him to start caring about money more than people, or to be corrupted."

Ryan nodded, understanding her dilemma far more than she could ever know.

"It will be his decision to make," he reminded her. "The terms of the estate are antiquated, so it can only pass to a male heir, otherwise the decision would have fallen to you or your mother, instead. But, allow me to tell you, Daisy, that you have a wonderful child. I'm sure, with your influence, he'll continue to grow into a wonderful man. Sometimes, the world needs people like that in charge of a privileged situation, in order to help others who could benefit."

She nodded, feeling conflicted.

"I suppose we should find out, either way," she said. "It would explain how we came by that lovely pocket watch, which Henry likes to play with."

"Yes, we saw it. He told us it had passed down your family."

"Yes," she said. "I assumed it was a gift from one of the baronets to my father, before he died, for many years of service as head gardener before Paul took over, and took over the house, as well."

She paused.

"I'm sure you've seen inside it," she said. "It never used to be that way, you know. When my parents had the place, everything was in good order. It's amazing how quickly things can go downhill, if you let them."

Wise words, Ryan thought.

CHAPTER 28

Jack Lowerson spotted Charlie's car as it pulled into her street and he took a deep breath, still not sure quite what he was doing there, only knowing that he couldn't be anywhere else. He and Mel had agreed to share their house as housemates, and he'd moved into the spare bedroom to mark the distinction, until they could decide what to do with the place and organise some of the practical details of their break-up.

Was it too soon? he wondered.

Possibly, but nothing was ever gained by being timid. As the thought entered his mind, he realised that Charlie had inspired it by being so inherently fearless, which he admired so much.

"Okay, Casanova," he said to himself. "Time to shine."

Jack let himself out of the car and crossed the road, words and sentences jumbling in his brain so that any erudite speeches he'd thrown together on the journey there now curdled to garbled mush.

He stepped up to her front door, and felt his stomach churn.

"Come on," he told himself. "You can do this."

He raised a hand and pressed the doorbell.

Endless seconds ticked by, until he heard fast footsteps approaching from the other side, and then it swung open.

"Jack," she said, and pulled in a tremulous breath.

He looked at her, taking in the soft, wavy hair she'd pulled into an easy ponytail so that she could go about the numerous tasks she accomplished every day. He liked to see her face, which was finely boned and dominated by a set of intelligent eyes, but the male part of him couldn't wait to unleash her hair and see it fanned out against a pillow.

"Jack?" she said again. "Is everything okay?"

There were words he could say, and wanted to say.

Apologies, promises, tenderness that lasted all through the day and night.

He continued to drink in the sight of her, feeling lighter than before, feeling free and ready to tell her how she'd changed him, lifted him, taught him and made him a better, happier man even in the short time they'd known each other.

But he said none of those things; there would be time enough for that.

"Do you feel the same way that I feel about you?" he asked her, softly.

She braced a hand on the wall, and took a deep breath. "That depends," she replied. "How do you feel about me?"

Jack smiled slowly, then, saying nothing further, stepped forward to cradle her face in his hands.

"I feel this," he whispered, before capturing her mouth in a deep, passionate kiss. In it, he poured his emotion, his admiration, his frustration, and she responded, meeting him with the same intensity, dragging his head closer to taste more, have more, *feel* more.

When they drew apart, both of them were breathing heavily.

"What about Mel?" she asked, racked with guilt at the thought of having betrayed her fellow woman.

"We broke up, earlier today," he said, and reached for her hand. "Will you give me a chance, Charlie? I can't stop thinking about you; you're always in my thoughts… you, and Ben. I can't promise to be perfect, but I can promise each day to keep trying to be better than the day before."

Tears began to fall, running in tracks down her face.

Then, she nodded.

"I thought—I thought you weren't interested in me, that way," she said.

"I'm very, very interested," he said, so there was no room for misunderstanding.

"I think we should take things slow," she said, as her eyes focused on the shape of his mouth.

"Me too," he said, and his hand came up to cradle the back of her head while she moved into his body once again. "Where's Ben?"

"With my mother, in the living room," she said, curving into the line of his torso. "Why do you ask?"

"I care," he said, and, in those simple words, won her heart.

"Can you—do you think you could love Ben?" she asked. "We come as a package."

Jack thought of the sweet, funny little boy with the rounded cheeks and downy soft hair, who giggled like a sailor and knew every kind of animal under the sun.

"I already do," he said.

"Jack?"

"Mm?" he said, moving her back against the wall. "Yes?"

"Don't break my heart, will you?"

He drew away so that he could look directly into her eyes, so she would know he was telling her the absolute truth.

"I will never knowingly hurt you, or Ben, or your mother, in any way," he said. "I'm human, so I'm sure I'll make mistakes, but not in big ways, not in ways that leave scars on your heart, Charlie. I'd never do that to you."

In answer, she smiled, and drew his head down into another kiss.

Ryan booked Mark Newman into his new accommodation for the evening, which comprised of a small, no-frills cell in the basement of Police Headquarters. He decided to leave him to percolate before questioning, and made his way back up to the main office suite. On his way upstairs, Ryan's phone began to ring a tinny rendition of an old Tears for Fears classic, and he saw that it was his mother.

Probably to ask him to pick something up, on his way home, he thought.

"Hi Mum," he said, continuing to make his way upstairs. "Is everything okay?"

"No," Eve said, in a voice clogged with tears. "You need to come home now, darling—"

He heard her suck in a ragged breath, and he stopped dead in the quiet stairwell, blood rushing in his ears while all kinds of scenarios ran through his mind.

"What is it?" he said. "What's happened? Is it the baby? Or Emma?"

"Emma's fine," Eve managed to say. "It's…it's Anna—"

The breath caught in his throat, and then his heart slammed against the wall of his chest in one hard motion.

Anna—

"She's been arrested."

He thought he had misheard. He must have done. "What did you say?"

"Anna's been arrested," Eve repeated, more slowly this time. "Some people from Durham CID came and took her away for questioning."

"On what charge?" he demanded, while his hand curled into a fist by his side.

Who dared arrest his wife?

When he found out who was responsible, he'd—

"They—they're saying it's murder."

Murder, his mind whispered, like an echo. *Murder, murder, murder.*

"It's a mistake," he said, in a funny, faraway voice. "It has to be."

What if it isn't?

"I'm on my way."

DCI RYAN WILL RETURN

If you would like to be kept up to date with new releases from LJ Ross, please complete an e-mail contact form.

AUTHOR'S NOTE

Belsay Hall and gardens is a real place, as with many of the settings I choose as the backdrop to my mysteries. Before I tell you about the few things I've taken the liberty of changing, I should say that the site holds a particularly special place in my heart—located only a few miles outside of Ponteland, it's very close to the place where I spent much of my childhood. I have fond memories of exploring the quarry gardens, or wandering the echoey rooms of the neo-Classical hall and its older companion, Belsay Castle, where events are often held for visiting families to enjoy and learn about some of the history of the place. It is very well maintained by the staff and volunteers of English Heritage (not to be confused with, 'National Heritage', the fictional entity I've created and used throughout this series as a nod to both English Heritage and the National Trust), whom I'll take a moment to thank, most sincerely, for all of their kind assistance. In particular, thanks go to Barbara Elder (whose name appears as a character in this story), and to Michelle, Bev, Susan, Lesley and Ged who, alongside many others, contribute to the wonderful care of this slice of Northumbrian history. Some of their names also appear, which, I hope, will bring a little smile when they read the story.

Now, onto the nitty-gritty.

The first thing to say is that, whilst I have tried to remain as accurate as possible in my descriptions of the site in and around Belsay, there are a few things I have embellished or changed slightly in order to fit the mystery. For instance, whilst the hall is indeed a fabulous example of neo-classical architecture, it is not, in fact, occupied or furnished, as you might find in some other English Heritage properties. The contents of the hall were dispersed at auction by the 9th baronet, Stephen Middleton, who, in 1962, decided to move to Swanstead, a smaller and more manageable house on the estate. Unfortunately, this meant that dry rot began to infest the main hall, which stood empty until it was taken into the guardianship of the state in 1980. Following this, a programme of repairs was undertaken, but visitors to the hall will note that it is displayed as an empty shell, in line with the guardianship agreement made between the family and the state. Nonetheless, it is possible to host occasional events in the pillar hall or atrium, such as a constabulary Christmas party, but I'm assured that a body has *never* fallen through the atrium window at any time during the hall's long history, so don't worry about that!

Now, a note on the Middleton family. You'll notice that I've created a fictional name for the inhabitants of the hall in my story—the Edgingtons. This is to preserve the fictional landscape, and as a courtesy to any remaining descendants of the Middleton family. Although the diary in the story was inspired by a real-life member of the Middleton family who was a noted diarist, the characters on these pages are entirely fictional figments of my imagination, and any resemblance to persons living or dead is entirely coincidental.

Belsay is a lovely place to visit on your own or with family, and I would urge you to see some of the architecture for yourself and to enjoy one of the cheese scones in the on-site café, located in the old kitchens, whilst reading a book from the second-hand bookshop located in the stable block, which has been put to good use as a welcome centre. The clock tower is very much real, and the clock is manually wound, as I've described in the story—the tunnel beneath the driveway is also real!

I'm sure I've forgotten to mention all kinds of things, but if you have any questions about the history, or feel the urge to follow in Ryan's footsteps, I encourage you to discover this gem for yourself and speak with one of the many helpful people who work there.

Until next time...

LJ ROSS
JANUARY 2025

ABOUT THE AUTHOR

LJ Ross is an international bestselling author, best known for creating atmospheric mystery and thriller novels, including the DCI Ryan series of Northumbrian murder mysteries which have sold over ten million copies worldwide.

Her debut, *Holy Island*, was released in January 2015 and reached number one in the UK and Australian charts. Since then, she has released more than twenty further novels, all of which have been top three global bestsellers and almost all of which have been UK #1 bestsellers. Louise has garnered an army of loyal readers through her storytelling and, thanks to them, many of her books reached the coveted #1 spot whilst only available to pre-order ahead of release.

Louise was born in Northumberland, England. She studied undergraduate and postgraduate Law at King's College, University of London and then abroad in Paris and Florence. She spent much of her working life in London, where she was a lawyer for a number of years until taking the decision to change career and pursue her dream to write. Now, she writes full time and lives with family in Northumberland

If you enjoyed *Belsay*, please consider leaving a review online.

If you would like to be kept up to date with new releases from LJ Ross, please complete an e-mail contact form on her Facebook page or website, www.ljrossauthor.com

Scan the QR code below to find out more
about LJ Ross and her books

There's a killer inside all of us...

After an elite criminal profiling unit is shut down amidst a storm of scandal and mismanagement, only one person emerges unscathed. Forensic psychologist Doctor Alexander Gregory has a reputation for being able to step inside the darkest minds to uncover whatever secrets lie hidden there and, soon enough, he finds himself drawn into the murky world of murder investigation.

In the beautiful hills of County Mayo, Ireland, a killer is on the loose. Panic has a stranglehold on its rural community and the Garda are running out of time. Gregory has sworn to follow a quiet life but, when the call comes, can he refuse to help their desperate search for justice?

Murder and mystery are peppered with dark humour in this fast-paced thriller set amidst the spectacular Irish landscape.

IMPOSTOR is available now in all good bookshops

SHORTLISTED
The British Book Awards
2020
BOOK OF THE YEAR

THE COVE

A SUMMER SUSPENSE MYSTERY (BOOK #1)

The perfect escape...

Gabrielle Adams has it all – brains, beauty, a handsome fiancé, and a dream job in publishing. Until, one day, everything changes.

The 'Underground Killer' takes his victims when they least expect it: standing on the edge of a busy Tube platform, as they wait for a train to arrive through the murky underground tunnels of London.

Gabrielle soon learns that being a survivor is harder than being a victim, and she struggles to return to her old life. Desperate to break free from the endless nightmares, she snatches up an opportunity to run a tiny bookshop in a picturesque cove in rural Cornwall.

She thinks she's found the perfect escape, but has she swapped one nightmare for another?

Suspense and mystery are peppered with romance and humour in this fast-paced thriller, set amidst the spectacular Cornish landscape.

"LJ Ross keeps company with the best mystery writers"
—The Times

"A literary phenomenon"
—Evening Chronicle

THE COVE is available now in all good bookshops